Steven Carroll was born in Melbourne. His first novel, *Remember Me, Jimmy James*, was published in 1992. This was followed by *Momoko* (1994); *The Love Song of Lucy McBride* (1998); *The Art of the Engine Driver* (2001), which was shortlisted for both the Miles Franklin Award in 2002 and France's Prix Femina literary award for the Best Foreign Novel in 2005; *The Gift of Speed* (2004), which was shortlisted for the Miles Franklin Award in 2005; *The Time We Have Taken* (2007), which won both the 2008 Commonwealth Writers' Prize for the South-East Asia and South Pacific Region and the Miles Franklin Award 2008; *The Lost Life* (2009), which was shortlisted for both the 2010 Barbara Jefferis Award and the ALS Gold Medal 2010; *Spirit of Progress* (2011), which was longlisted for the 2012 Miles Franklin Award; and *A World of Other People* (2013), which was shortlisted for the South Australian Premier's Award 2014 and was co-winner of the Prime Minister's Literary Award 2014. He was a finalist for the Melbourne Prize for Literature 2015. *Forever Young* (2015) was shortlisted for the Victorian Premier's Literary Award 2016; and the Prime Minister's Literary Award 2016; and *A New England Affair* (2017) was shortlisted for the Victorian Premier's Literary Award 2018. *The Year of the Beast*, the sixth novel in the Glenroy series, was published in 2019. His novel *O* was published in 2021.

Steven Carroll lives in Melbourne with his partner and son.

Also by Steven Carroll

O

Praise for *O*

'[The original] *Story of O* has now been superbly transformed ... the new *O* is told with warmth and imagination, its intelligence acute and its ethics irreproachable'

Judith Armstrong, *The Sydney Morning Herald*

'enthralling, beautifully written ... a compelling new interpretation'

Katharine England, *The Advertiser*

'an intelligent, earnest, searching novel'

Geordie Williamson, *Weekend Australian*

'Carroll's portrayal of this remarkable woman is both respectful and intelligent, a gripping reimagining of this time'

Anna Carew-Reid, *Sunday Times*

'Carroll has done a spectacular job. *O* is beautifully written ... a heartbreaking love story'

Readings

'immensely powerful'

Good Reading

Praise for *A World of Other People*

'*A World of Other People* is a powerfully imagined, elegiac homage to love, heroism and poetry ... an intimate private drama, set against the immense and tragic backdrop of European civilization tearing itself apart'

Prime Minister's Literary Awards judges, 2014

'A fine, absorbing novel – darker than *The Lost Life* but equally eloquent and assured. Carroll's re-creation of a distant and now long-lost world is vivid and tactful'

Andrew Riemer, *The Sydney Morning Herald*

Praise for *The Time We Have Taken*

'Carroll's novel is a poised, philosophically profound exploration ... a stand-alone work that is moving and indelible in its evocation of the extraordinary in ordinary lives'

Miles Franklin Literary Award judges, 2008

'The result is a deeply satisfying encounter with the empty spaces that the suburb failed to fill both between people and inside them. Carroll takes time to tell an untidy story with a gentle sense of wonder. His prose whispers loud'

Michael McGirr, *The Age*

'It is the creation of a larger concept of suburban life in all its transcendent possibilities that makes this novel so special. Carroll's revelations of these beautiful insights into our utterly ordinary world make him a writer worth cherishing. His prose is unfailingly assured, lyrical, poised'

Debra Adelaide, *The Australian*

Praise for *The Gift of Speed*

'Carroll's gift for evocative storytelling ... had me captivated'
Australian Bookseller & Publisher

'A novel of tender and harrowing melancholy'
Le Nouvel Observateur

'Carroll's a rare beast in that he writes with great affection and understanding about life in the suburbs ... A lovely rites of passage novel that is oh so carefully crafted and captures the evanescence of time to perfection'
Jason Steger, *The Age*

'Carroll's writing is astonishingly assured'
James Bradley, *Australian Book Review*

Praise for *The Art of the Engine Driver*

'Subtle, true and profoundly touching'
Le Monde

'A veritable gem ... a beautiful discovery'
Elle France

'An exquisitely crafted journey of Australian suburban life ... fresh and irresistible'
Miles Franklin Literary Award judges, 2002

'A little masterpiece'
Hessische Allgemeine

Praise for *The Lost Life*

'Carroll's prose is limpid and assured ... [a] poised and beautifully burnished work. Carroll's control is masterly'

Andrew Riemer, *The Sydney Morning Herald*

'This is not so much a departure as an arrival ... Carroll's fiction is distinctive for the way his clean prose decelerates experience, puts aside the urgings of linear temporality, to reveal a richness that habitually evades us'

Australian Literary Review

'Carroll's prose has a sublime rhythmic quality ... almost as if he has sung the words on the page'

Australian Book Review

Praise for *Forever Young*

'No Australian author has better evoked the sense of change, the ravages of time, the obligation to self as well as to others. *Forever Young* is on one level about nostalgia, without ever succumbing to it ... At every turn this exquisitely crafted novel can widen our notion of what it is to be human, then, now and, possibly, later'

The Sydney Morning Herald

'The title of this fine novel speaks ambivalently to a longing for lost youth, and to the desire to escape its sentimental claims'

Peter Pierce, *The Australian*

'Carroll ... transmutes the grey facts of daily life into light and luminous art'

Geordie Williamson, *The Australian*

Praise for *A New England Affair*

'This is a languid, angry, heart-rending novel, thoughtfully layered and passionately expressed'

The Australian

'Carroll has carved out a stark and simple portrait of yearning, stripping away any dizzy glamour of the role of an artist's muse to present a far sadder and more pragmatic study'

The Saturday Paper

'As always with Carroll, it is … the richness of ideas, the allusive, measured prose, the subtle cross references to other books and literary theories that captivate the reader'

The Adelaide Advertiser

'Carroll's quiet, measured style is imbued with breathtaking observations of seemingly small moments. His writing here invites contemplation and reflection on what we lose in life and what we have, who we think we are and who we aspire to be. This novel is so much more than the sum of its parts and it's impossible not to feel you have borne witness to something incredibly beautiful and true'

Victorian Premier's Literary Award judges, 2018

'It is a deeply moving, intense and poignant novel of a love that never finds the right moment'

Mildura Midweek

Praise for *The Year of the Beast*

'a notable work; it covers many ideas, and personalities, showing the complexities of apparently ordinary lives, and places them convincingly in the context of larger social and philosophical issues. *The Year of the Beast* ends the Glenroy sequence while remaining true to Carroll's sense that history is always with us and within us, human propensities never change, and stories never really end'

Dennis Haskell, *The Age*

'There's much to enjoy here: the convincing historical fabric of Melbourne during the Great War ...; profound observations of the human condition; the humanity of the two main characters ... and their resistance to and emancipation from an oppressive moral code.'

Good Reading

'Steven Carroll's Glenroy series [is] one of the most ambitious undertakings in 21st-century Australian literature so far – a century long in chronological scope, a suburb wide in its intimate domestic attentions ... He has taken a few generations of ordinary women and men ... and made an epic of their lives. They live and breathe in these hundreds of pages. They are purely human: flawed and beautiful in their flaws'

Geordie Williamson, *The Australian*

'written with a perfect poetic pace ... Melbourne is Carroll's city and it is through this new novel, this seamless, delicious read, that he presents a story of our home to us, and for us. A rare gift indeed'

Christine Gordon, Readings

'a wonderful book, richly evocative of its time and with unforgettable characters'

ANZ LitLovers

Goodnight, Vivienne, Goodnight

Steven Carroll

FOURTH ESTATE

Fourth Estate
An imprint of HarperCollins*Publishers*

HarperCollins*Publishers*
Australia • Brazil • Canada • France • Germany • Holland • Hungary
India • Italy • Japan • Mexico • New Zealand • Poland • Spain • Sweden
Switzerland • United Kingdom • United States of America

First published in Australia in 2022
by HarperCollins*Publishers* Australia Pty Limited
Level 13, 201 Elizabeth Street, Sydney NSW 2000
ABN 36 009 913 517
harpercollins.com.au

A catalogue record for this book is available from the National Library of Australia

ISBN 978 1 4607 5111 4 (paperback)
ISBN 978 1 4607 0574 2 (ebook)

Cover design by Lisa White
Cover image © Richard Jenkins
Author photograph by Rebecca Rocks
Typeset in Berthold Baskerville by Kirby Jones
Printed and bound in Australia by McPherson's Printing Group

CONTENTS

WEEK ONE

Late July, 1940

1.

Leaving With the Laundry

The September sun was wasted on them as they walked about the deck, Tom and Vivienne. Southampton, 1932. A date etched in her diary. She, one moment, talking about the piano lessons she'd just started and trying to sound as though nothing out of the ordinary was taking place, and that he wasn't going away to the other side of the world for a year, from old England to New England. The next minute tugging his sleeve, an insistent child, saying, '*Must* you go? *Why* must you? Tell me again. There's something you're *not* telling me. What? Tell me!' On and on, a sudden, exhausting barrage of questions. For both of them. Moods rising and falling like the slap of the waves against the side of the liner. Vivienne the waves, Tom the imperturbable liner.

Vivienne. Vivie. Viv. Now distant, now near. Who was she? The Vivienne now sitting in the gardens of Northumberland House, Finsbury Park, is contemplating the question. A fellow inmate in a floral dress sits on a garden bench, waiting for someone who never comes. He didn't yesterday or the day before, nor will he come today. Who was that distant Vivie? Who, indeed? Timid, withdrawn, vulnerable and silent one moment, a storm the next, all over you with endless questions. Pure energy, a force of nature, then all energy spent and wrung out, withdrawn and silent again. Delicate Vivie, always a nervy girl, a bundle of maladies and pain the doctors could never explain. Her father's delight, her mother's burden. Poor Vivie, poor Tom. Poor everyone for that matter.

Shoulders slumped as they continued to walk around the deck, she stopped tugging his sleeve and was suddenly talking about the new maid. Didn't trust her. Shifty look. And all the time, Tom not saying much. Seventeen years together, and most of it nerve-rattling silence or screaming battles. He always thought more than he said. And on the deck that day what should he have said? It wasn't for a year, but forever?

No, anything but that. This was no time for the truth. He couldn't have coped, she couldn't have. Who wanted a scene? It's no way to say farewell. Except it wasn't farewell, it was goodbye. She *must* have known, that other Vivienne, that distant one. Surely somewhere in her worn-out, aching bones, even if she didn't admit it, she knew what was going on. But how do you tell yourself that when it's the last thing you want to hear? So they walked, and talked, and stepped around the truth.

All too soon, or at last – depending on which of the two you were – they heard the announcement for visitors to leave the ship. At the gangplank she turned; they kissed and hugged. No great fuss, no lingering. Husband and wife, for the last time. Only she didn't acknowledge it then. She waved from the dock, leaning against her brother, Maurice. Good old Maurice. Father understood her, Maurice was learning to. Tom waved from the railing. He might even have been smiling. Why wouldn't he? Free, at last. But Tom would never be free, especially of the past. Fact is, freedom scared the living daylights out of him. And there he was, sailing into it.

Then everything slipped away from her, faster than she expected, and Tom was wrenched from her. She *felt* it. And still does, as though a hand had reached in and torn some vital organ from her. Bloodied and hollow, gasping from the blow and the pain, Maurice's shoulder propping her up, she watched from the dock until the liner was a blur on a flat sea, puffing smoke from bright red funnels into a clear September sky, the horizon never so vast, the world never so empty, the day never so long. Still she waved. Not that she could see Tom, or he her. If, indeed, he was even standing at the railing anymore. The wave was for herself.

Vivienne has gone over that scene time and time again. At first, cursing herself for not having the stamina or the courage to go with him. The sea is not her element, and she fears ships. Doesn't trust them. Ships are no match for the sea. The sea will always win. So she didn't go and she has spent these last eight years wishing she had. But you can only go over things so often. Now – sitting in this funny farm they put her in, because, well … what with all the waiting and not hearing from Tom and not knowing *what* was going on or where he was and everybody against her, and the days so long and the sleepless nights dark and endless … things really did get out of hand – she knows it wouldn't have made a scrap of difference anyway. His will was made of iron, his heart the same stuff. It wouldn't have mattered what she said or did. Iron thoughts went with him. Besides, you can only go over things so often, until you just don't care anymore.

No, that's not right. It's not that she doesn't care: part of her, and a large part too, the best of her, will always care. How could she not? Seventeen years is seventeen years. It's not that she doesn't care, it's just that the heart, like a lonely child waiting for the mummy and daddy who never turn up for a school visit, can only wait so long before it has to face facts and leave the waiting room alone. No, it's not that she doesn't care, she's moved on. Had to. It was move on, or die. It had to stop. And one day, when she felt her waiting heart would burst, she told her heart to be still. Cease to yearn or she would be forever yearning for what was already lost. Let be, and just *be*. And let what comes come.

She never thought she'd have it in her to do it. Nobody did. But when a wound cuts deep, the pain has to work its way out in its own time. Slowly, agonisingly. Not to be rushed. For its leaving will only occur when the moment is ripe – like the day, the very second, that a marriage ends. But when the moment comes, and the pain is gone, you find it's not only the pain that's moved on (like a restless spirit to find another body to inhabit), *you* have too.

Her body changed as well. Auntie stopped visiting. That's what her mother called it. Have you had a visit from auntie? Has auntie come yet? Auntie was always visiting, at odd times. You couldn't tell when auntie would drop in. She was there on their wedding night. What a night, stripping the sheets from the bed and washing them in the bathtub, while Tom sat saying nothing. But not long after they brought her here auntie stopped coming, and she knew she'd never have to worry about auntie again. These things, she knows, affect people differently. For herself, the moment auntie ceased to come she felt her whole body relax, and a soothing peacefulness flowed through her. And slowly, neither one Vivienne nor another, but a mixture of what was and what was slowly emerging, her world started to change. She slyly stopped taking the medication they gave her and stopped telling herself that if she could only get to the bottom of this or that, everything would be all right. Stopped it all, and let come what might. She was moving on, and she could feel it.

A miracle, a gradual one, no sudden awakening. Just a wide shadow line, days blurring into months, and months into years. And when she'd finally traversed that shadow line, in a sort of slow motion, she looked back and waved to the distant, ghostly Vivienne she once was: the woman in all the cramped flats they ever lived in; the one at all the awful dinners, sitting in silence one minute then screaming at Tom or the whole table the next; the forsaken wife on the dock that day he left. And that distant self waved back, saying go now. You have earned this. There's nothing for you here, we have detained each other long enough. He's not coming back. No one to wait for. Do not pin your hopes on the wrong things, for they are the wrong hopes. Go now. If anybody has earned this, you have. Go.

And so one evening in the garden of this place they brought her to, she finally turned away from the past and moved on, watched by the moon in thoughtful repose. A miracle. A mystery. One she may never understand. The mind saying move on, and the body, no longer resisting, slowly came together – mind and body operating in concert, in the very depths of her, out of everyday sight, beyond sonar or searchlights – and together they performed some secret ministry, and brought about a miraculous metamorphosis that delivered her into a new life. As the fog slowly lifted she knew, beyond doubt, that she was perfectly sane.

It's a beautiful morning and Vivienne is waiting for a friend. Well, not a friend exactly – but her friend's friend. Somebody called George is coming to pick her up and take her out of this place. In a laundry van. Her friend, quite possibly her only friend, thought of that. Louise. Louie. A good, clever friend. Vivienne knows perfectly well she's sane, and so does her friend, but *they* don't. And she knows she'll never convince them. No point even trying. So she's going to give them all the slip: the doctors, nurses, gardeners and the receptionist who sits in the front office, watching over the comings and goings of the institution. A laundry van drives in, a laundry van drives out. No great mischief. Not, she imagines, until lunchtime, when someone will say, 'Have you seen Mrs Eliot?' She laughs. It's impossible not to.

There's a war out there. Another one. It happened when she had other things on her mind. Planes pass overhead, lumbering bombers and the darting small ones. What do they call them? Spitfires. Huh. Isn't that what her father called her? Or was it Maurice? It's still strange to think that her father's not here anymore, not anywhere anymore. The two men of her heart, Tom and her father. But of the two, it was only her father who really loved her. Or understood her. This she can see now, quite clearly.

There was a dog-fight over this part of the city yesterday. Strange word, 'dog-fight', conjuring up some conflict in the constellations between the boar and the hound. But yesterday's dog-fight was real. The whole of Finsbury Park stopped what it was doing and looked up – cars came to attention in the street, shoppers paused, the gardener froze in mid-prune. A plane fell from the sky in flames and the gardener cheered, as you would at a football match. She'd gazed at him as he resumed pruning the roses, saying over and again to herself, they call this man sane. Just as they call that world out there sane.

There are no planes in the sky this morning. Nothing to tell you the world has gone to war. Not here. Northumberland House. Sounds like a country manor. Looks like one. Except for the white coats. The wheelchairs, and the occasional screaming from a ward or treatment room. She takes in the gardens, the greenhouses, the inmates around her, sitting in the morning sun. The middle-aged woman in the floral dress has a handbag on her lap. She's dressed as if for an outing. She always is. And the handbag is always on her lap. As if she's expecting to leave this place any moment. Occasionally her lips move, speaking to no one. If this woman were the subject of one of Vivienne's father's paintings she'd be called *Lady with a Handbag*. She clutches it as if the handbag were hope itself. Her mornings pass in expectation of a visit. Or is it simply a way of feeling normal? Does it make her feel the way she used to before whatever it was that came along and broke her spirit? Vivienne's heart goes out to this woman, and not for the first time. It was one of those signs that told her things had changed. Your heart goes out to a stranger and you know that your world has widened. The view is different: not inward-turning but outward. Your sorrow is no longer for yourself, but someone else. And with a sudden pang she realises she's going to miss the Lady with a Handbag, although they've hardly exchanged a word over the years. She asked her once what she thinks when she stares out over the garden, sometimes for hours, and she said, 'Why do you ask? What do *you* think?'

Just then she hears a nurse speak to another woman a little further away. Mrs Williams, the nurse is saying, your husband is here. The woman looks at the nurse, as if to say, who? Your husband, the nurse says again. He's here. The nurse takes the woman's hand and leads her to a man sitting on a bench under a lattice arch. The man has a felt hat in one hand and a small bouquet of flowers in the other. He is a picture of love. He is in love with this woman, but she has forgotten who he is. Or perhaps she sometimes remembers and a rush of old love passes through her. How splendid it must be, Vivienne thinks, to hear those words. 'Mrs Williams, your husband is here.' Tom has never visited her. Not once. At first she waited: sad, angry, baffled. But then she realised he never would. And the heart can only wait so long … Perhaps that was when the fog started to lift. When it finally sank in that she would never hear those splendid words, 'Mrs Eliot, your husband is here.'

She checks her watch. Almost time. The laundry van will be here soon. She rises and slowly walks back to her room. A sort of small one-room villa really. Detached from the main building. Maurice liked it. Her mother calls it cosy. She would. Always on the look-out for her little Vivie. Nervy Vivie. Distant Vivie. The ghost she once was. She steps inside, sits and waits, remembering the night they brought her in, at the same time wondering if she really does remember it or has just pieced it together from what everybody told her afterwards. Mrs Eliot, found wandering the streets at five o'clock in the morning by a fresh-faced young police constable. Is it true my husband has been beheaded? They're after him, there's a plot. I must save him. Did she really say that? She's been told she did. Often enough. Or is it one of those memories of something you never did but imagine you have? But why would the constable make that up even if he had the imagination? Maybe it was

Maurice, or Tom? What's certain is that the young constable found her and led her to the police station. Yes, he must have. Her doctor, summoned from his sleep, asked her who the prime minister was and she told him it was a silly question. The prime minister, whoever he was, was of no importance to her so *why* should she know his name? Wrong answer. There were all sorts of other questions – she remembers this much, or thinks she does. Questions, questions, to which she gave the wrong answers. Must have. She finished up here, Maurice and her doctor speaking soothing words that she can't remember now. Just that they were soft, soft as a conspiracy.

She sits on the edge of her bed and looks around her room. There are so many things she will simply have to leave. Three years of things. And it occurs to her with a curious pang that she might even miss this place too. Funny farm or not, this is where she got her mind back. And, at this moment, it's almost as though she thinks of it as a retreat, a place to withdraw from the blows of the world. This is where that miraculous thing occurred. This is where she said farewell also to her pain, that ache that was always there with varying degrees of severity every morning and which left her bedridden for days on end. It threatened to kill her, but in the end, did it *make* her? This is where she learnt to love that pain and thereby, perhaps, released it. All she knows with any certainty is that release did come, for her body as well as her mind. And it wasn't what the doctors or nurses said, or the drugs they gave her, which she only ever pretended to take – for after a lifetime of doctors and drugs she'd had enough of all that. No, *she* did it. Nervy Vivie, delicate Vivie. Somewhere in the depths of her being she found something. Something strong she never knew was there.

And all the things she accumulated along the way, the stories she wrote or half wrote while she's been here, the letters and cards from her mother and Maurice, and Louise, who dreamt up this whole crazy scheme, will have to stay behind. And although she'll miss these things and all the other little knick-knacks that she can't take with her, she knows it's right they should remain. They constitute the old life. A new life awaits. A second chance. It is an end, and a beginning. The old life is baggage. Except, she suddenly decides, her stories, all those tales finished and unfinished. Yes, she'll take them, she tells herself, and tucks the notebook into her coat pocket. She has left the door ajar. Soon, somebody called George will step in and they'll find out if the plan works. She stares at the door. Not long now.

* * *

'Mrs Eliot.' She hears him before she sees him. He steps in and closes the door quietly, speaking softly, almost in a whisper. 'It's time.'

George, brown hair parted at the side and receding at the front, looks a solid type, just like his name. And a big man too, which is just as well. He looks around her room, photographs and prints on the walls, books by the bed, a colourful shawl draped over a chair.

'You can't take anything with you, you've been told?'

She manages a smile. 'You make it sound as if we're crossing into the afterlife.'

'Well,' he says, matter-of-factly, 'let's call it a new life.'

'I'm just taking this,' she says, revealing a tortoiseshell cigarette holder. 'I've become rather attached to it. Oh,' she adds, 'and my notebook.'

He nods, holding open a large canvas laundry bag. 'All right, but we need to go, right now. Here,' he tells her, an air of concern and sympathy, 'you'll have to crawl in. I'll put your sheets and towels on top of you. Quick. Don't be frightened.'

Vivienne gives the room one last look, a silent farewell, then crawls into the laundry bag and curls up. She feels the sheets, towels and pillowslips fall on her. Then she is hoisted up and airborne, bouncing out the door, indeed just like a bag of laundry.

George is whistling, a good, clear, confident whistle. Sometimes a whistle is a giveaway, sometimes it's just right. George's is just right. It's a rich whistle too, musical. Even she could believe that nothing out of the ordinary is taking place and that the bag really is just full of laundry. He greets one of the gardeners and comments on the morning, no hint of strain in his voice. Then she hears the back doors of the laundry van being opened and George places her inside, sliding the bag across the floor. She hears him chatting with someone, then hears the thud of a bag being dropped in. Then another, and another, until he closes the doors and locks them into place.

He starts the engine, they move. It's a warm morning, and the air inside the bag is heavy. She breathes harder, sucking in the oxygen. Soon she is sweating, and the bag seems to amplify the beat of her heart. She doesn't like to hear the sound of her heart, never has; she'd rather it just got on with its job without her noticing. But she's got no choice, and she's beginning to wonder how long she can stay cooped up with the washing.

When she hears George cheerily chatting to the receptionist from the driver's seat she knows they are at the front gate. There is some talk about where the regular driver is. Off sick, says George. Nothing serious. Cheerio. Lovely morning.

Then the van eases forward and they draw out onto the road, gathering speed as they go. So fast. She could almost laugh. It's happened. It really has. She just left with the laundry. Like a scene from a farce or some Christmas panto. But it's real. They drive on for a few minutes more, then the van pulls to the side of the road. She hears the back doors open, and feels the morning sun coming in.

'George?'

'Mrs Eliot.'

'Here, George. Here.'

Then the bag is opened, the towels and sheets on top of her are flung away and she pops her head out.

'Not so bad,' he says, with a hint of a grin as she gulps in the air.

'No, not so bad.'

'Small price for freedom.'

He helps her out of the bag and she stands up. Yes, he seems to be thinking, a petite woman. 'Ah,' she says, 'my holder,' as she ferrets about inside the bag and retrieves it.

'Done?'

'Done.'

'Here,' he says, taking her hand, 'come and sit up the front.'

'Is it safe?'

He nods. 'We're a good mile from the home. It's safe.'

When she slips out the back of the van and steps onto the road it's as though she's never seen this particular sun before, this particular sky. And as much as she'd like to just stand there and take the moment in, she can't. George opens the passenger door and swiftly helps her up. Then they're off again, and this time she does break into laughter, a loud shriek of a laugh. She covers her face, laughter exploding from her, delicious sunlight striking her eyes.

'We *did* it!'

George smiles. 'We did, Mrs Eliot.'

'You did well, George.'

'So did you, Mrs Eliot.'

'That whistle. My God, *I* believed it. You ought to be on the stage.'

He gives a sly smile. 'As a matter of fact–'

'I knew it. You're an actor!'

'Of sorts. Amateur. When I can. I'm what they call a man of parts. Odd jobs.'

'Splendid parts.' She grins, tucking her feet underneath her. 'Was I heavy?'

'Light as air, Mrs Eliot. You surprised me. Light as a feather.'

Her face becomes pensive. 'I've felt like a feather all my life, George. Being blown about.'

'But not today.'

'No,' she says, the smile back.

It is only when she turns from George and looks out the window at the buildings they are now passing that she notices the sandbags at the front of a post office. And the windows of shops and houses, taped up. Little box cases slung over people's shoulders and uniforms in the street.

'Of course,' she murmurs, 'the war.'

'You wouldn't have noticed it much inside.'

'We had an air-raid shelter. Two, in fact. But no, not much. The odd,' she reflects, pausing, 'dog-fight. Why do they call them dog-fights?'

'I don't know. Never thought about it.'

'I have. They're not dogs, they're young men.' She dwells on this a moment, then turns to George. 'And you, they haven't put you in uniform yet?'

'Me?' He laughs. 'I'm a bit old for that.'

Of course, she hadn't thought of that. It's been a big morning. 'How old are you, George?'

'Just turned forty-nine, Mrs Eliot. Too old for this one and too young for the one before. So I'm an air-raid warden. I'm the one who tells everyone to close those curtains or else.'

She smiles, she can just hear him. 'That's almost my husband's age,' she says, vaguely registering a certain strangeness about the words 'my husband'. 'Have you heard of him? Everybody has. Every time I opened the door or picked up the phone somebody was asking for him. Never me. You *must* have heard of him, but say you haven't. You don't have to mean it. I give you permission to lie. Say, I've never heard of T.S. Eliot.'

'I've never heard of … who was it again?'

'That's very good, George. Correct response. There are times when I wish I'd never heard of him. But there's no point wishing you've never met someone when you have, and no amount of wishing will change things, will it?'

'No.'

'No,' she repeats wistfully. 'It's more complex than that. It always is. Besides, this is the first day of …'

She trails off, and George turns briefly to her.

'Of a whole new life, Mrs Eliot.'

'Yes.' She nods. 'I was afraid to say it.'

'Don't be afraid.'

'I'm afraid that comes naturally. I've always had this fear that when things go well they'll soon go bung. That it'll all be snatched from me.' She stares intently at George, a question forming. 'How do I *sound*, George?'

'What do you mean, sound?'

'Do I sound all right?'

'Yes.'

'Don't sound, well … odd?'

'No.'

'My voice, it sounds normal to you? A lot of people don't like being called normal, as if it's not good enough. But that's *all* I want. Just to be normal.'

'You sound fine, Mrs Eliot.'

'Fine?' She shrugs, as if to say: I'll take that. 'And if you met me, I mean if you met me just anywhere sometime, some place normal, the way people meet, you'd think I was fine?'

'I would.'

'Ready for the world?'

'Ready for the outside world, Mrs Eliot.'

She rests her head back on the car seat, determination in her eyes. 'You betcha!' she says, affecting a Midwestern drawl. 'Pretty darn ready, all right. Waited long enough, too darn long. But is the world ready for Six-gun Vivie?' She snaps out of the game. 'My husband's American, did you know that? A Missouri man.'

'No, I didn't. He sounds so posh.'

'It's an act.' She pauses. 'How do you know how he sounds?'

'I heard him on the wireless. He's a bit like Winston Churchill these days, he's everywhere. Didn't you know?'

'No,' she says. 'Nobody tells me anything.'

They fall silent, George concentrating on the road, Vivienne looking out the window, taking in this strange new world. Strange – she gets her mind back; the world loses its. But it's her world all the same. And it's been out here all the time, all through the lost years, waiting for her to step back into it. A greeting at the ready, like an old friend or a faithful servant. Welcome back, Mrs Eliot.

She turns round to George, curious and eager.

'Where are we going?'

'Harrow.'

'Harrow? Is that really necessary?'

'I'm afraid it is, Mrs Eliot.'

'Vivienne.'

'Vivienne.'

'That's better. I haven't really been Mrs Eliot for some time now. What's in Harrow?'

'A safe house. It's where you'll be staying for the next thirty days.'

'Why thirty days?'

'That's the law. Stay out for thirty days and you're free.'

'Yes, yes,' she says thoughtfully. 'That's what Louise told me, but is it *really* the law? Can it really be true?'

'Good question, Mrs Eliot. We haven't got quite that far yet. There *is* an old law that says if you can break out of an asylum and stay free for thirty days, which proves you can look after yourself, they can't make you go back. So they say.'

She sighs. 'The mysterious "they".'

'It's a sporting country, Mrs Eliot, and everybody deserves a sporting chance. If the fox can outsmart the hounds, then the fox goes free.'

'And whom will I be staying with?'

'Me. My sister. It's her house. We're part of the Society, Mrs Eliot. The Lunacy Law Reform Society.'

* * *

The Lunacy Law Reform Society. While the laundry van makes its way across London, George explains the Society to her. Could be someone's idea of a joke, she thinks, or the title of a matinee comedy. But you couldn't make that up, and from what George says nobody was joking when they formed it a few years earlier.

All volunteers, from all parts of the city. Lawyers, nurses, doctors, teachers, artists of one sort or another and the occasional odd-job man like George himself. Serious-minded, humane, solid – good people on the whole, but not above breaking the law. For if you have to break the law to change it, then so be it. The Society, George adds, befriends people inside and springs them from asylums and stows them away in safe houses all over London. Those that shouldn't be there, that is. Mrs Eliot's friend, Louise, and a good and loyal friend too, said Viv shouldn't be there. Viv was nervy, Viv was a handful and Viv was once quite mad – all things considered, who wouldn't be? – but she's not anymore. She's as sane as us. So what's she doing in there? Everybody agreed. And that was when the plan was drawn up and George was called in to put his acting skills to work.

The rest of the journey passes in a sort of daze, Vivienne marvelling at being in the world once more. They cross the city – Finchley, Cricklewood, Harrow – until they pull up at an ordinary two-up, two-down suburban home, and Mrs Eliot is delivered into the safe house, and the safe hands of the Lunacy Law Reform Society.

* * *

'Welcome, Viv!'

Vivienne looks round, a touch of wonder in her eyes, at this small group she has fallen in with – Louise, who has just welcomed her, George and his sister Marjorie – and can't help but feel she's in the company of a bunch of outlaws. Not in a forest, but the depths of suburban Harrow.

But if they are outlaws, they are outlaws with excellent manners. Everything is quite formal. Louise kisses her on the cheek, Marjorie shakes her hand, welcoming Vivienne into her house, and even George shakes her hand as if meeting her for the first time.

'Lovely day,' says Louise, with a wide smile.

'You haven't spent half the morning in a laundry bag.'

'Small price to pay for your freedom.'

'That's what George says.'

'George is right. Some plans work.'

'Some do.'

She's known Louise for years, and in that time she's barely changed. From the start she always struck Vivienne as a sort of ageless girl guide. One of the seniors. Organising everyone, and very good at it. Someone born for the role. And her clothes, plain skirts and tops, nothing showy, not exactly a uniform, but like one all the same.

It's then that Louise acquires a secretive, even sly, smile as she gazes at Vivienne.

'Would you believe we've got a little surprise for you?'

'Today, I'll believe anything.'

Louise walks towards a closed door. 'It's just a little thing.'

With a dramatic flourish she flings the door open, and a small silky brown terrier flies through the opening, ignoring everyone else in the room and darting in a direct line straight for Vivienne.

'Polly!' she cries as the dog leaps, and she scoops it up in her arms. 'Oh, Polly.'

The gathering in the sitting room beams as mother and child are reunited, the dog wriggling then settling into the crook of her arm. All trust. Vivienne eventually looks up, wiping her eyes, then hugging the dog. 'Sometimes I think I missed this little dog more than Tom. Or anybody for that matter. Where has she been?'

'She's been house-hopping,' Louise says, then adds, 'We thought you'd like some company.'

'You thought well,' Vivienne says, still holding Polly as though, like everything else, the dog was not quite real. 'And you seem to have thought of everything.'

'We tried,' says Louise. 'All of us.' Her manner becomes serious, even strict. 'I may not be able to come here again after this morning,' she adds, a touch of the spy chief explaining the rules of the game.

'Why not?' Vivienne asks, concerned that her friend is concerned.

'I'm your chemist,' Louise says sternly. 'They know this, and the moment they discover you're gone, and they surely will have by now, they'll come looking for me. May even follow me.'

'We have to be very careful,' Marjorie adds. 'For thirty days. After that, if the law works the way we all hope it does, you'll be free.'

'But not until then,' Louise says. 'Do you think you can do this?' she asks, as if, it seems to Vivienne, and she has to smile, her friend is asking her if she can make a fire with flints and sticks. But there's also that hint in her question that Vivie has always been unpredictable, and the clear implication that during this time she'll have to play by the rules.

'Of course. That's why I'm here.'

'I can't stress this enough,' Louise says matter-of-factly, a let's not get sentimental tone. 'We have to be very careful.'

'But I can go out? Don't tell me I can't go out. Surely you can't expect me to stay caged up here all the time.'

Louise, Marjorie and George look at one another in silent consultation. 'Sometimes,' says Louise at last. 'But don't draw attention to yourself. It's unlikely they'll be looking for you out here. But who knows?'

'Little trips. That's all I need,' Vivienne pleads. 'The tube. Who's going to know? I haven't been *in* the world for a long time. I want to see it. And I'll be invisible, I promise.'

'Of course, there's a lot you want to see,' Louise says, then pauses and gathers herself. 'But Viv, we have to try very hard. Don't we?' she adds, this time in the manner of a concerned mother talking to a wayward child. For although she is certain that Vivienne is as sane as any of them now, she has had years of talking to and negotiating with the fragile, the exhausting, Vivienne, who fired question after question at her; the Vivienne who was found wandering the streets at five in the morning by a police constable, asking about the beheading of her husband – the Vivienne who was always fragile and who went mad for a while.

Vivienne, still cradling the dog, stands as tall as her petite frame allows. 'I *know* that.'

Dignity? Or is it pride? Both? When you've been robbed of them for so long, been spoken to like a sad, bright child (too much keen insight for her own good; pull the wool over her eyes and she pulls it straight back again), like a firecracker about to go off, like a mad woman who is exhaustingly mad to the point of sanity – when you've spent a lifetime being spoken to like that, pride and dignity are often the only things you've got left to cling to. Signing her letters 'Mrs T.S. Eliot', announcing herself at parties and dinners as Mrs T.S. Eliot, shouting at the secretary at Tom's work and saying do you realise you are talking to Mrs T.S. Eliot? – that was the last of her dignity, the shreds of her pride, speaking.

A way of saying, of telling everyone, all those friends who turned their backs on her, that everything was as it was and always had been – that Tom hadn't walked out and *was* coming back. Any day now. He'd just walk in the door as if he'd never been away, and smile. A way of saying his home was just waiting for him when he came to his senses and all those so-called friends of his stopped pouring poisonous lies into his ears: his wife, the dog, his old umbrella leaning against the hallway stand, infinitely patient and loyal, were all just waiting for him.

She can hear Louise's voice, then Marjorie's as well, both discussing her, what Vivienne must and mustn't do, but at the same time they've become distant and she's drifted off to an afternoon in the garden of the home … was it a year ago?

Louise and Vivienne were chatting. About nothing much in particular, when Louise stared at her and said, 'You've changed.'

'Have I?' she said.

'You know you have.'

'Yes, silly me. Of course I have. How, do you think?'

Louise paused for some time, then finally said, 'You're calm. Peaceful. Serene's too strong a word.'

'No, I don't do serene.'

Louise nodded. 'Quite frankly, you're the last person I would have thought capable of it, and I say that as a friend.

But you remind me of someone who after years of waging war with life, every day a new battle, has declared peace.' She had said this with both conviction and curiosity. And it was then that she added, happily, jauntily, 'You're sane, you're perfectly sane, aren't you?'

And, more sure of herself than she had ever been, Vivienne looked straight back at her and said, 'I'm as sane as you or anyone else out there.'

With that Vivienne fell silent and the conversation closed. But that was when Louise started making plans. And, in time, she quietly let Vivienne in on the secret. At first it sounded preposterous: a sack, a laundry van. But the more Vivienne thought about it, the more she observed the comings and goings of the home, the more she could *see* it. Some plans work.

Even so, there is a distinct air of unreality about being here. One of those dreams that you eventually wake from, when your sleeping consciousness tells your sleeping self, oh, it's a dream. But as much as she's been waiting for that waking moment to announce itself and the balloon to burst, it hasn't. And here she is.

'Are you listening?' Louise asks, breaking into her thoughts. And again she tells Vivienne that they all have to try very hard, in that tone they all used to adopt – her mother, Maurice, Tom, the whole bunch of them – when talking to that other woman she used to be. And as Louise talks to her, the old need to assert herself arises, like a reflex, and she summons again all her pride and dignity and stands tall.

'Yes,' Vivienne says, putting the dog down on the floor, 'I'm listening.'

Louise nods, looking her up and down.

Vivienne knows what Louise is thinking: that she's sane, but still edgy – and who wouldn't be? How many go to the brink? How many come back from it, the sensation of teetering on the edge never far away?

'We'll meet weekly,' says Louise. 'But not here. I'll call, from a phone booth, and I'll let you know.'

'What sort of meetings?' Vivienne says, intrigued, the hint of a smile in her voice.

'Briefings. Just so you know what's going on.' Louise looks at her watch. 'Now I must go to work,' she says. 'I leave you in good hands.' She glances at Marjorie and George. 'The best of hands.'

She kisses her friend's cheek. 'Bye, Viv. For now.'

Vivienne kisses her back. 'Bye, Louie. And watch out for that awful other woman who everybody mistakes me for, and who always gets me into so much trouble.'

'*Got* you into trouble!' says Louise. 'Not anymore.'

2.

The Detective as Biographer

Detective Sergeant Stephen Minter gazes up at a blue morning sky, clear except for a few puffs of cloud. A gentle breeze, a warm sun, the smell of freshly mown lawn. Cricket weather.

He picks up a small handful of grass clippings and throws them into the air, gauging the direction of the breeze as a bowler might before a match. He owes a lot to cricket: it was his gateway into a new country, his family having arrived from Austria in the summer of 1930 when he was thirteen years old. Jewish, but you'd never know it. They never went to synagogue. And Minter is one of those names that could be anything. He was never given any one reason for the move, apart from being told that Europe was a mess and England would be better.

Not that it was ever an issue with Stephen, for from the moment they docked, stepped off the ship and took a bus through the green summer countryside to London, he felt inexplicably at home. Right from the start. He couldn't explain it then, and he can't really satisfactorily explain it now. But it came with a certain anxiety – like falling in love with a girl you imagine is out of your league – that intensified the child's natural instinct to fit in. It is all very well to fall in love, but how do you make the object of your love fall in love with you?

The answer he hit upon straightaway was cricket. The bus paused in a village where a match was in progress. White figures on a round, green field. He was transfixed, for the very movements of the figures on the field seemed to be part of some design. He could sense that much. There were rules, there had to be. And he determined, intuitively, that the game held the key to fitting in. If he could just learn what those rules were, then he could understand this new country of his, and woo it. It was, he later reflected, the order of things that he loved most about the place. And this game seemed to be the very picture of that order. Not that he thought of it like that then. The feeling came first. The words came later.

The bus moved on, but the image stayed. And the first thing he did when he went to school in London, his father having set up shop as a tailor in the East End, was learn those rules and play that game, in the firm belief that it would open all those schoolyard doors that all new boys need to open. And he was right. For he discovered that he was very good at the game. That it came as naturally to his body as the feeling of being at home. Play the game well, and everybody will cheer and you will be home.

But he always had a touch of the loner. Still does. He played *in* a team. But not necessarily *for* the team. Truth was, he played for the cheers. Something he knew, but which anybody looking on wouldn't.

The game, the rules, the order, the country. It was as though some deep craving had been satisfied, and he felt instantly that he had landed precisely on that part of the earth he was destined for. And it was that love of his adopted country that led him into the army when war started and took him to Norway, to Lillehammer, where a German bullet shattered his knee on his first day and left him with a permanent, painful limp. He'd walked from the police force into the army in 1939, and limped from the army back into the force when he got out of hospital. Promotion. His own office. Spoils of war.

With the memory of bright summer days and green fields, and with the smell of lawn clippings all around him, he lowers his eyes from the sky to the asylum gardens and turns to the nurse beside him.

'When did you notice she was gone?'

'Yesterday. Morning tea. Somebody said have you seen Mrs Eliot? And I said no. It was odd. She likes her morning tea.'

'When did you last see Mrs Eliot?'

'At breakfast, or perhaps here in the garden later.'

'How did she seem?'

'What do you mean?'

'Well, was she happy, sad, normal?'

The nurse pauses for a moment. 'Not sure "normal" was ever the word for Mrs Eliot,' she says. 'Let's say there was nothing out of the ordinary.'

'No signs?'

'Signs?'

'That she was planning something.'

'Nothing.'

Stephen stands, hands in coat pockets, looking round the garden, greenhouse nearby, air-raid shelter a little further on. He turns towards the front gate of the home.

'That the only way out or in?'

'Yes. For this part of the home. It's large.'

'I can see that. But let's assume that's where she left.' He eyes the office and reception area overlooking the exit. 'She didn't just walk out.'

'She couldn't have.'

'She had help.'

'Must have.'

He scans the gardens again: a woman with a handbag on her lap; a man and woman sitting on a bench like a husband and wife in Hyde Park; a gardener trimming the roses.

'Where was she based?'

'This way,' the nurse says, pointing to a row of small units just beyond the garden. 'She had a room to herself. Some of the patients do.'

'So she has money?'

'Someone does.'

The nurse pushes the door open and they step inside. Stephen strolls about the room – a fair size, washbasin, mirror – and raises his eyebrows, nodding. An exotic scarf is draped over the mirror. He opens the drawers. All full. Make-up, books, framed photographs – all where they seem to have been for a long time. The overall effect is that the occupant has just stepped out for a few minutes.

He takes one of the photographs from a small table and looks at the nurse.

'This her?'

'Yes. The little one, not the tall one.'

He examines the photograph. Three people stand in a garden – a tall, thin woman, a besuited man with an enigmatic smile, and a small woman, head bowed, in a white dress. And straightaway the word 'fragile' pops into Stephen's head. She's in the photograph but gives every impression she doesn't want to be. No, it's not that she doesn't want to be, but as though she's not wanted and knows it.

'This Mr Eliot?' he says, pointing to the man in the middle.

'Yes.'

'And the tall woman?'

'Mrs Woolf.'

'The writer?'

The nurse shakes her head. 'I don't know. Mrs Eliot just told me that's Mrs Woolf, as if I ought to know the name.'

Stephen contemplates the scene, puts the photograph back on the table, and picks up another. It is Mrs Eliot, but younger. Much younger. She sits on a bench, another garden. Smart striped dress, and she's leaning forward towards the camera, the hint of a smile on her face, eyes sharp, as if about to interrogate the photographer. She's confident, even cleverly provocative. And daring. Someone who says the things that other people only think. At least that's how she comes across. The word 'fragile' does not occur to him now – only, as he contemplates the two photographs, the question: what happened between one photograph being taken and the other?

'If you don't mind I'll keep these.'

'No, I don't mind.'

He rests the photograph back on the table with the others for the moment and looks up.

'Any visitors?'

'Not many. Some.'

'Who?'

'Her brother occasionally.'

'Name?'

'I've forgotten, sorry. He'll be in the visitors book.'

'And?'

'Her mother. Not lately. She's frail.'

'Father?'

'Dead.' She pauses. 'Oh, and a friend, a chemist from up the road.'

'A friend?'

'Yes. She didn't have many.'

'Her name?'

'Louise. Can't remember the rest.'

He glances back at the photographs. 'And Mr Eliot?'

'He's never visited.'

Stephen concentrates his gaze on the nurse, taken by surprise. 'Never?'

'I've never seen him. Nobody has.'

'A bit odd, wouldn't you say?'

'They're separated. He left her. She never got over it. It seems.'

'And that's why she went ...'

The nurse raises an eyebrow, mentally finishing his sentence. Is that what brought her here? Possibly. The final straw, who knows?

'What was your impression of Mrs Eliot?'

'What do you mean? Professionally or personally?'

'Both.'

'We're not meant to have personal opinions.'

'I'm very good with secrets.'

She weighs her words. 'Professionally, she is ... was ... difficult.'

'How so?'

'She was all questions. One on top of the other: Why did you say that? What do you mean? What do you all mean? I never know what you mean, tell me ...' A slight shake of the head. 'She was exhausting. After ten or fifteen minutes you were drained. Although,' she stops, reappraising this, 'not so much lately. She's been a lot quieter recently. Almost peaceful.' The nurse pauses again, reflective. 'She's bruised and brittle. Made you sorry for her. She could tell, and it got her back up.

She doesn't like people feeling sorry for her. She's hard to like, if you want to know. Almost made it impossible to like her. I can only imagine what she was like to live with.'

Stephen nods, taking the nurse's words in, then turns his attention back to the room, reopening and closing drawers, until he comes to a bundle of small black books. Two are chemist-shop diaries. Boots. One is a Selfridges diary. He flicks through them, entries both regular and irregular in pencil and ink, a mixture of neat writing and messy, frenzied entries, ink splotches all over some of the pages, the writing all but impossible to read.

'I'll take these too,' he says.

The nurse shrugs. She says nothing, the shrug says it all, as if she would dearly love to shrug Mrs Eliot off her shoulders.

Stephen pockets the photographs and the diaries and turns to leave.

'I'll need the names and addresses of the visitors.'

'They're in the book.'

'And this chemist friend, Louise—'

'Purdon,' the nurse breaks in, suddenly remembering.

'Do you think she'd try anything like this?'

'I doubt it. Always struck me as a bit of a square.' She pauses, remembering something else. 'There is this group. I've heard about them, that's all. They call themselves the Lunacy Law Reform Society, or something like that. They spring people from places like this.'

'Do you have any names?'

'Heavens no. I don't think anybody does. Apart from them, of course. They're a bit like the Scarlet Pimpernel.'

'Lunacy Law Reform Society?'

'Something like that.'

Stephen scratches his head. Who knows? They could be behind this. The nurse closes the door and they walk back through the garden to the office – the woman with the handbag now gone, the husband and wife departed, the garden trimmed. The smell of lawn clippings still in the air, the sky clouded over.

* * *

Stephen is listening to his superior talking about Mrs Eliot. He's been summoned to his office to discuss his visit to Northumberland House.

'She's not just any missing person, Minter, this is Mrs T.S. Eliot. You've heard of him?' says his superior, a man in his early sixties who, just a year ago, had been looking forward to retiring.

'I know him. But I haven't read much of him.'

'Neither have I. Not the point.' His boss suddenly stops, staring at Stephen quizzically. 'Did you say "much of him"?'

Stephen nods.

His chief is tossed between being impressed and being suspicious. 'He's not just any poet, Minter. He's a public figure. Part of the war effort. Think of him as a kind of Winston –

who can actually write. Well, so they say. He's got support in important places.'

'I appreciate she's a missing person, sir. And that's unfortunate. But thieves and crooks are having a picnic out there at the moment ...'

His chief breathes in and lights his pipe, smoke and words issuing from him simultaneously. 'Do we really want the spectacle of Mr Eliot giving a speech, reading his poems – and people flock to see him, believe me – and suddenly having to deal with his mad estranged wife, screaming from the audience for him to come home? Or worse?'

Stephen gives the slightest flick of his eyebrows, a suggestion that this might be awkward, but awkward isn't urgent.

'No, sir.'

'No.'

There is a silence, his boss puffing on his pipe, Stephen waiting to be released.

'He's reading to the royal family next week. Then in halls and colleges all over the city. Society women, they love him. And the troops. Not just toffs. Ordinary people turn up to his readings. People look up to him. He makes them feel proud. He makes them feel intelligent. Heaven knows, people need someone to look up to.' A slow white cloud rises from his boss's desk. 'Your job is to find her.'

'London's a big haystack, sir.'

His boss nods. 'But your needle is out there somewhere. Drop whatever you're doing. We'll give you a car. You'll need it.'

'A car?' Stephen raises his eyebrows, impressed and aware that it shows. 'Thank you, sir.'

'I thought you'd like that,' his chief says, then pauses. 'You can drive, can't you?'

'Yes, sir.'

'The leg?'

'Not a problem.'

'Good.'

'But, sir … she might have scarpered. Be hiding in the country. Left the city. Where's her home? Where's she from, sir?'

'No idea. You've got some homework to do.'

Stephen shrugs, the slightest hint of annoyance.

'Just find her,' his boss says with an air of finality, then smiles and dismisses him.

Stephen returns to his desk, picks up Mrs Eliot's diaries and flicks through them, looking for something that might help. But they're nearly all about Mr Eliot. Tom. Where he is. What he's doing. Why he hasn't come home. On and on. No great help.

He stares out the window on to the street scene below. A car? That's something. The army taught him to drive, but he never thought to actually have a car. He grins. Exciting. All the same, he'd rather not be stuck with the job of finding Mrs Eliot. Rather not drop what he's doing. While the country's going to war, thieves are going to work. And he'd dearly love to catch a few of them rather than a middle-aged woman who's probably no threat to anyone.

* * *

It's odd. Or perhaps not. The way that if you're not looking for something you just don't see it. However much it may be under your nose. But once you start to look or become aware of something, you see it everywhere. Or think you do. Like superstitious people – and who isn't? – who are stalked by the number thirteen.

Stephen's train, in fact, entered the station at 10.13. Not that it bothered him. But what he does notice now whenever he stops and gazes into a bookshop window is Mr Eliot. He seems to be everywhere. He fills the windows – his books, and this sort of pamphlet with the curious title *East Coker*. And as often as not, his larger-than-life photograph is staring out at you, following you, a haunting sort of presence.

Stephen is headed for Somerset House. Records. Births, marriages – the inevitable. He could have got off the train at Temple, but he's stubborn. Always been a good walker. He enjoyed the beat before the war. Covent Garden was one of his old beats and it feels good to be in the footsteps of his younger self. It reminds him of how he used to be. How he used to feel. And so, limp or no limp, he's decided to hoof it down to Somerset House.

And, of course, there's a bookshop on the way. A big one. And its window is filled with this same green pamphlet, the words *East Coker, East Coker, East …* stretched from one side of the window to the other. Impossible to ignore. Stephen steps

40

inside to buy a copy. He reads poetry, but not a lot. And he has read some of Mr Eliot. He likes to read, not something he lets on about at the station. His mother was an English teacher in Austria, and perhaps some of her love of reading rubbed off. Most of all he reads novels, sometimes even the odd detective tale, just so he can pick holes in it. But today he's buying poetry. And he's not the only one. There's a queue. When he steps back onto the footpath he's holding both the pamphlet and Mr Eliot's collected poems. He puts them in his army rucksack, then continues on his way, occasionally wishing he'd brought the walking stick they gave him at the hospital.

* * *

Born: Bury, Lancashire. May, 1888.

Stephen looks up from the birth certificate of Vivienne Haigh-Wood and takes in the gloomy reading room of Somerset House, this old palace somebody once called home. There are three others poring over fusty documents in the dim light. Like characters from Dickens, Stephen decides.

He has a notebook resting on the desk and jots down the basic facts. Bury, 1888. He makes a quick calculation. Current age, fifty-two. Father listed as a painter. Mother, mother.

He puts the document aside and reaches for the marriage certificate. June, 1915. Hampstead Register Office. Home address, 3 Compayne Gardens, Hampstead. He smiles; so much for Bury. Can't blame her. And Mr Eliot? Address, Oxford

University. Of no occupation. Born in St Louis, Missouri, United States. Father, a brick manufacturer. Missouri? Stephen stares at the word, feeling drawn to the name, registering the faint impulse that, one day, he might like to see Missouri – and the realisation comes that the country's great poet, who fills the windows of bookshops and libraries, is not even English. No, he's from St Louis; she's from Bury. Both twenty-seven. Bit old. Perhaps they were fussy. Too fussy. Perhaps they arrived at each other via other loves that never amounted to what they promised. A marriage of second choices. Second best. Each bringing a ghost to the marriage.

And Hampstead Register Office at six in the morning. No parents. One aunt as witness. Hasty? Secret, even? It's almost as if they eloped. He stares at the document, the inescapable feeling that between every line is a story, either bursting to get out or hiding there in silence, hoping nobody notices. There is ample room on the certificate to contain the short version of the couple's lives, but – and here the young detective sergeant asserts himself – detail is always welcome.

He reaches for the final document, the death certificate of Mrs Eliot's father. Charles Haigh-Wood. Painter. 1854–1927. Stephen gives a slight nod: fair age. He looks over the three documents one last time. Nothing more to concern him. He closes his notebook, pockets it, and returns the documents.

Outside, the summer sun is warm. Sky clear. Pleasant afternoon. He barely notices the sandbags stacked against the buildings, the barbed wire, the taped-up windows of the shops, the soldiers, sailors and occasional flyers on the footpaths. Amazing, how quickly one gets used to these things. How soon they become normal.

Above all, his mind is probing the bare facts. A story either bursting to get out or hiding between the lines in silence. The facts are all very well. The place we start from. But it's the story behind the basic facts that he wants. Stephen has always thought of detective work as a kind of storytelling. You play with one story, then another and another, until you come up with one that feels right. Feels true. Then you test it.

So what's Mrs Eliot's story? Father an artist. Unusual. Not a sideline, but his job. He's personally never heard of him, but Stephen's hunch is that he did well from it. The shift from Bury to Hampstead suggests as much. Compayne Gardens. He's not familiar with the area. Not his beat. But it sounds, if not posh, well off. Comfortable. Hampstead, after all. He can almost picture the scene. Father, a successful painter. Mother, always there for her two children. A light, airy house. Large garden. Secure childhood.

But none of that fits with a marriage at a Register Office at six in the morning – especially with no parents present. Almost an elopement. Why? One set of facts, two stories. One conventional, or giving that impression; one not. Whichever story is true, in the end it led to an insane asylum, an escape and a missing Mrs Eliot.

Stephen comes to a stop at the Covent Garden square. No market today. He's suddenly aware that he must have been lost in thought, and he's thankful that he was, because it's only when he stops and looks around that the pain in his knee reasserts itself. And with it that voice calling 'Get down!' A split second after hearing those words he felt the shattering pain in his knee as if a bomb, not a bullet, had hit it. His legs fell out from under him and the skirmish went on without him until the reconnaissance party returned and carried him into the town. Lillehammer. What was left of it. What was left of his knee. Wouldn't be padding up next season, or any other.

Could have been worse. Could have been clean bowled first ball. Never troubling the scorers. Next thing he was in a hospital outside of Hastings. Lillehammer, not going back there fast.

But he wasn't aware of the ache for a while there, and he's got Mrs Eliot to thank for that. As he crosses the square he notices a sort of art gallery-cum-shop. Not large, but solid and reputable looking. A well-dressed elderly gent smiles as he enters. Stephen closes the door and is immediately aware of a kind of calm and peace falling on him. It's one of those quiet, hushed places that inspire quiet conversation.

'Good morning, sir,' the man says. 'How may I help you?'

'I haven't come to buy.'

'Not many do. Not these days.'

'Just thought you might be able to tell me something.'

The man gives a slight shrug. 'What's that?'

Stephen takes his notebook from his pocket and opens it. 'Have you heard of a painter called Charles Haigh-Wood?'

'Of course,' the man says.

'Then, he's famous?'

The man makes an equivocating gesture with his hand. 'Well known. He was once very fashionable. He did ...' the man contemplates his response, 'domestic scenes. Mostly ladies in pretty dresses. That sort of thing. But not bad. They were often reproduced as greeting cards. We have one.'

'Here?'

'Well, not the actual painting. A print. He still sells.'

The man leads Stephen to the back of the shop and stops in front of a large framed print. There are two children in the image, a girl and a boy. There is a book, pages torn from it, lying on the carpet of what looks to be a very comfortable, well-appointed house. Just the sort he'd imagined.

'It's called *The Peace Offering*,' the man says. 'It's one of his well-known ones.'

He steps closer to the print and points. 'That's his daughter. And that's his son.'

'His daughter?'

'Yes. They've had a fight. The boy's giving her an apple. That's the peace offering.' The man pauses a moment, gathering his thoughts, almost, it seems to Stephen, like a gallery guide. 'He's from that time when paintings often told a story.'

Stephen says nothing, gazing wide-eyed at the print. At the painter's daughter: curly fringe, flushed cheeks, frilly, beribboned clothes. The future Mrs Eliot. Just a girl. About ten or eleven. And as he stares at the painting, he can feel himself being drawn into the story.

The man, noticing the extent to which Stephen is absorbed by the painting, speaks.

'You like it?'

'In a way.' His voice is vague. 'But I can't afford it.'

'We have it as a card. Pocket size,' the man says, going to the front desk and returning with a card reproduction of the painting. 'Here, have it.'

'But …'

'No cost. Have it.'

'That's very kind of you.'

'A pleasure – hope I've been of help.' He smiles. 'Good morning.'

It is a sort of dismissal, and Stephen returns the salutation as he steps out of the shop and back into the square, where he stands examining the card. The future Mrs Eliot. Just a girl. But a very pensive one. A few hours earlier he wanted only to be rid of the case; now he feels the tug of the tale.

And what's more, the ache in his knee was gone the whole time he was in the gallery. Strange thing, the mind, he tells himself, as he limps back to Covent Garden station.

3.

The Peace Offering

'I'm going to read you a story.'

'I don't like stories.'

'You'll like this one.'

'No, I won't.'

A girl about ten or eleven, prettily dressed in the pretty clothes of another time, is sitting on a stool in front of a fireplace. A boy, three or four years younger, is standing in front of her. There are paintings on the wall behind them, richly coloured rugs and carpet, and it's not difficult to imagine a window looking out on to a garden.

The girl looks the boy up and down.

'You have to sit down.'

'Why?'

'Everybody sits down when they're being told a story. That's how it is.'

'I don't want to.'

'I'm older than you. You have to do what I say. That's how it is too. Daddy's older than Mummy, and Mummy listens to

Daddy. Mummy's older than me, and I listen to Mummy. I'm older than you, and you do what I say. Now, sit.'

She says this with such force and conviction – indeed, like a child queen from a storybook – that the boy sits down cross-legged on the carpet.

'Now,' she says, 'let's begin.'

The boy, all restless energy and resentment, wriggles on the carpet, looking out the window on to the garden. The girl, resting a coloured picture book on her lap, starts. It is her favourite story, the tale of a young girl called Alice. She's not sure what she likes most, the tale or the coloured drawings, particularly of Alice, with her blonde hair and her blue ribbon. For she not only likes the look of Alice, she wants to *be* Alice. So it's not only her favourite story, it is, in a sense, *her* story. Alice, in the tale, is lounging on a river bank with her sister and is bored, when she suddenly sees a white rabbit with pink eyes go by. Nothing unusual. But when the rabbit mutters something about being late, the boy interjects.

'That's stupid. Rabbits don't speak.'

'This one does.'

'How?'

'It's a story,' she says, as if that alone is sufficient explanation. There is silence. The girl, queenly indeed, gathers herself, and the tale of Alice and the rabbit resumes. But when the rabbit takes a watch from its waistcoat pocket, the boy erupts again.

'That's stupid too.'

'No it's not. It's,' and here the girl pauses, summoning the right word, 'imaginative.'

'Rabbits don't wear clothes or have watches.'

'You have to use your imagination. Do you *have* an imagination?'

The boy, sensing that he is being accused of some deep deficiency, fires back at his sister. 'Of course!'

'Then use it.'

Wriggling and angry, he sits and listens, if only to prove that he does have this grown-up thing called an imagination, and for some time lets his sister read on without interjection. In fact he seems so attentive that she is lulled into a false sense of security. But when Alice drinks a magic potion and shrinks to a tiny ten inches, the boy leaps to his feet.

'That's *too* stupid. It's all stupid. Why do I have to listen?'

'To find out what happens.'

'I don't care what happens.'

'Stop!'

Her voice rises, loud, almost a shriek, and the boy's voice rises with hers. They are shouting.

'The story's stupid.'

'The story's not stupid – you are. You stupid little boy.'

'I'll show you who's stupid.'

With this the boy snatches the book from her and rips a handful of pages from it, scattering them on the floor.

The girl springs from her stool – it is not only her favourite book in pieces on the floor, but the picture of the girl she wants to be. 'You vile, stupid little boy!' she shouts. 'Look what you've done.' Then, with all the authority of an outraged queen, she shrieks, 'Pick the pieces up!'

'Pick them up yourself.'

The girl is beside herself. She would dearly love to scratch his eyes out.

'Vile little child!' she screams, disappointed with herself for not being able to think of something different or even worse, the words not having the same force the second time round.

And with this, sensing that the queen's authority is weakened, the boy bursts out laughing. The girl, wearing her new, strong, stout leather shoes, and with murder in her eyes, kicks the boy square in the shins. One leg, then the other. The boy screams in pain; the girl keeps kicking, never satisfied. She could murder her brother. *Really* murder him. And the boy, clasping his shins, manages to kick his sister back. She screams, the door flies open, and suddenly their father is standing there.

Such is his authority that Charles Haigh-Wood doesn't need to speak. Silence falls upon the room. The girl is in tears. The boy is standing to attention. The father surveys the scene: the torn book, the two children facing each other in a stand-off.

'Maurice,' the father says, 'come with me.'

Without protest, the boy follows his father out of the room. They remain outside, talking in the hallway, for some time, the girl listening and catching a phrase here and there. She makes out the word 'delicate' more than once, and she knows they are talking about her.

When they re-enter the room her brother is carrying an apple. Watched by his father, he walks up to his sister and offers it to her.

'What's this?' she says, in no mood for apples or anything from her brother.

The boy, as if quoting from a book or repeating lines he has memorised, says, 'It's a peace offering. Because Vivie is very delicate. And if I'd been to hospital as much as Vivie, I'd be delicate too.'

The girl ponders this for a few moments, then looks down at the carpet.

'Pick up the pieces first.'

This is too much for the boy, who has already swallowed his pride and given up his dignity, and so he turns to his father, defiance in his eyes.

The father sighs. 'Leave the book where it is. Maurice, stay standing with the apple in your hand. Vivie, sit back on the stool. Stay perfectly still, do not move, do not speak.'

He leaves the room, is gone for a minute or two, the two children staring at each other in unspoken accusation: you did this; no *you* did. When their father re-enters he is holding a sketch pad and pencils. He pulls up a chair, sits and begins.

'You will stay like that until I have finished. Do not move, do not scratch or wriggle.'

This, clearly, is their punishment. To stay like statues until the sketch is finished. Furthermore, implied in their father's instructions is the threat that if they move he will have to find other punishments.

And so they sit and stand, staring at each other in silent fury. What is more, their father seems to take pleasure in lingering over the sketch and extending their agony. At one point the boy raises his arm to scratch his nose, but lowers it quickly the moment he catches his father's eyes. At the same time, his sister remains perfectly still. If this is a game, she is better at it.

It seems as though the whole morning has passed and the best part of the day is gone when their father finally looks up, then closes the sketch pad. He contemplates his children anew.

'Now, Maurice, pick up the book and the pages you tore from it, and put them on the table.'

The boy hands the apple to his father to hold while he performs the task, then does as instructed.

'Good,' the father says, handing the apple back to the boy. 'Now, offer the apple to Vivie.'

The boy extends his hand to his sister, the apple nestled in his palm.

'Now, Vivie,' the father continues, 'accept the apple.'

The girl, noting that her instruction to pick the book up has been carried out, finally accepts the peace offering.

'Good,' the father says. 'Now let that be an end to it. Off you go.'

The boy bolts immediately, and is soon running round the garden.

The girl goes to the table and picks up the torn pieces of the book and tries to put them back together again.

* * *

The finished painting is in a public art gallery now. At Bury. Vivienne never saw it after it left their house, and she doesn't want to. She turns on the Hampstead footpath she has been lingering on these last few minutes and leaves the old house, her childhood home, where she and her brother grew up – if they ever did. If anybody ever does.

The fact of the painting now being in an art gallery always strikes her, when she thinks about it, as a kind of violation. And strangers staring at it, a kind of intrusion. Like strangers rifling through your letters or diaries. Or going through your drawers, like thieves. The painting depicts a private moment that now only she and her brother *really* know. Or should know. Her father long dead. It is a private moment, now on public display. A spectacle to which strangers bring their prying eyes, making of it the utter nonsense that people make of these things. The painting tells a story, and there can only be one true story. And the thought of people gaping at the painting, at the private moment it depicts, is like standing naked in a crowd. Feeling their eyes on you. Or as if your most private thoughts were on public display. For every Tom, Dick and Harry to know. No longer yours. Nothing private.

No, she has never visited the Bury Art Gallery, nor will she ever. She'd have to go back to small-town provincial Bury, for a start. And mingle with the people. Then mingle with those who stand and gape at her father's painting. No, it's too much.

She enters the station, sky blue above her, her gas mask over her shoulder. Everybody carrying their masks. Masks, masks everywhere. She's not used to it yet, but everybody else is. It's another sunny day, the platform a mixture of cheery laughter, stoic faces and posters asking if your journey is really necessary. But what still preoccupies her is the thought of herself and her brother, up there on the wall of an art gallery. Forever. In the end, that's what art comes to. Private moments given over to strangers to ogle. The most intimate moments pinned and wriggling on the walls of galleries.

Or in the pages of books. She knows all about that.

4.

Sibylla and the Fête Galante

A woman called Sibylla is arriving early for a party. She wants to be early; she doesn't want to arrive late and be gawked at. Her friend is protesting: arriving at a party early is so déclassé. Their talk is urgent and clever, the way talk never is in life. Only on the page. Or at parties like this, full of clever people. They enter the house and are ushered into a large room where a few guests have already assembled. What now?

Sibylla approaches an American financier who's leaning against a mantelpiece. But he's not leaning casually. He's struck up a pose, a transparent one. All the same she approaches him and says hello, but he only smiles. With his flat hair plastered to his scalp, his thin red lips and bulging black eyes, he should be ugly, but she likes him.

Sibylla is in most of the stories Vivienne writes. Sibylla *is* Vivienne. More or less. And the American financier? Well, Tom did work in a bank. Despite herself, despite his exaggerated pose, his lugubrious eyes, Sibylla likes him. If only he'd … what? The question is left dangling on the page. For now.

Vivienne puts her pencil down, leaving her notebook open. She'll continue her story later. Sibylla and the American financier. A wave of tiredness has swept over her, her energy drained by the last few days and the trip out to Hampstead. Tired, she's tired, and at five in the afternoon she's ready for a nap. Even feels a bit weak. Might have caught something.

No, she's just tired. Has been all her life. Her natural condition. She sighs. It's a miracle she ever had the energy to write anything. But she did. And Tom *was* good. Read them, liked them, published them. Well, most of them. Not the ones she's writing now. When she's got the energy. She sighs again. Why, why is it always such an effort? She likes putting the pen to the page, forming words, lovely words, and gradually creating a story. And what's more she's good at it. Doesn't just think she is, she knows she is. And that's what Tom said too. But it's always such an effort. So draining. Leaves her weak.

She settles into an armchair that faces the window, the dog curled up beside her in its basket, the soft sounds of the street outside filtering into her thoughts. More memories than thoughts. Sensations past, but still with her. Hospitals, hospitals, hospitals … She closes her eyes. The house is silent, the dog wheezes in its sleep. A drowsy numbness creeps over her; the house, the room, the street outside all slip from her …

Strange smells are in the air around her. Scary ones. And white, everything is white: the walls, the big lights, the tag on her wrist. She's lying on her back being wheeled somewhere, staring up at the ceiling, five or six years old. A man in white with a white mask is talking to a woman in white. Someone else is pushing this trolley she's on. Her mother and father are there somewhere, and she wants to get up and go home with them. With Mummy and Daddy. But she can't. She's on wheels and somebody is pushing her far away from everything she knows, deeper and deeper into this strange, frightening, smelly white world.

When they stop there are lights everywhere. Strong ones. She squints. White walls, white lights. Where have her parents gone? She can hear the doctors talking about her, about what they're preparing to do, using strange, frightening words, not lovely ones. She doesn't know what they mean but she doesn't like them. Mummy and Daddy said she must be very brave, and so she is. She'll be brave for them. And Mummy will love her more than Maurice. She clings to this thought as a man in white puts something over her face. More strange smells. He is quietly telling her that she's going to have a pleasant little sleep. Just like an afternoon nap. Does she still have an afternoon snooze? Sometimes. Well, she's just going to have an afternoon snooze. Isn't that nice? And when she wakes up Mummy and Daddy will be there. Mummy and Daddy will be … Mummy and Daddy … Mummy …

Perhaps that was her first time in a hospital. Must have been, everything so strange. Her first operation. But it all became quickly familiar. And all she's left with now of those early years is a blurred memory of being in and out of hospital all the time. The same one, or maybe not; they were all the same in the end. She had something called TB. In her bones. They had to get to her bones and for that she had to go to hospital and be very brave. And she was. Everybody said so.

Her eyes are heavy; there is a distant voice in the street outside. She really can't recall the first time a doctor gave her a little something to make her feel better. To calm her down. Because Vivie was showing signs of becoming a nervy girl. She never knew what this little something was; she didn't need to. It was just called Vivie's medicine. Vivie was just a little girl. Her doctors told Mummy and Daddy what to do, and Mummy and Daddy told Vivie. That's the way things worked.

The TB went, but not the delicate, nervy Vivie. Hospital-case Vivie. She seemed to get everything. Whatever there was to be got, she got it. And after a while, it was hard to know what came first. The nerves then the sickness or the sickness and the nerves. Round and round and round they went, one chasing the other, then being chased.

The dog snorts, Vivienne rouses herself, looks about her, the room bathed in late afternoon light. She rises and sits at the small table she's been writing at, her notebook where she left it, and gazes down on the street. A young soldier stands in front of the tobacconist's, lights up and breathes in deeply. He strolls off. A carefree air. Something she's never known. Does he know how lucky he is? No, of course not. If he did, he wouldn't be so carefree.

As he disappears she picks up her cigarette holder, puts in a cigarette and lights up. There is a bottle of whisky on the table by the window. She never used to drink; why would she? She was always bathed in ether or some other alcohol. She drank through the pores of her skin. Now she's off drugs. Has put them aside. Let come what will. No more drugs. The whisky, though, is a present from Louise. The next best thing to having her friend here. But, of course, she can't be. That would be careless. Vivienne knows that. All the same, there are times, especially during this late part of the afternoon, when friends should gather, that she wishes Louise was here. Louise took a big gamble on her, and so when Vivienne raises her glass it is as much to her friend as to freedom.

Tom liked his whisky. Still does, no doubt. And she's momentarily distracted by the thought that had things unfolded differently, they might have lived to enjoy a whisky together at this hour. Just like some normal couple. But that's just it – they were never normal. She shrugs, is anybody? She draws on her cigarette, she sips the whisky. The street scene below changes, thoughts come and go. Mostly of Tom.

Early, very early in those mad few weeks that you might call their courtship, they were walking through Soho one evening. Tom and Viv. They did that sort of thing then. Did things together. Everything was exciting. Tom telling her about his midnight walks back home in Boston. In Paris. And now Soho. The two of them. The world they walked through transformed by the night. Wonderfully strange. A world apart. Street lamps, like rows of yellow moons come down to earth, hummed and glowed as if transmitting some secret communication to them. Throwing up symbols and images. A world inhabited by drunks, prostitutes, stray animals – all the night's creatures. Together they possessed it, Tom and Viv, collecting their images and filing them away. A treasure trove to be drawn upon when the time came.

They were the good times, the best of times. Easy to remember because there were precious few of them. When they shared everything, and spoke without thinking. Everything an adventure. Good to know the good memories are still there, she tells herself, drawing on her cigarette, after everything. For she finds it difficult now to remember much at all without this draining, deep sadness coming over her. The way a sudden cold or flu does. What a time, what a time we had … She looks out over the street. All good one minute, then gone bung the next. The memory of it now like strolling through an old battlefield: the sounds of fighting, the shrieks, the hurtled words, long since faded. The quarrels that caused the ruptures long forgotten. She draws once more on the cigarette, the dog curled up in its basket. No more sad tales. There's too little time left to be taken up with sad tales of kings and queens, and those that we took for gods, who turned out to be all too human in the end. No, no more sad tales.

The scene outside has slipped into early twilight, and down in the street people are going about their Friday evening business. There's laughter, shouting and talk: ordinary people reaching out towards a little bit of living, ready to let loose. Life! Right in front of her. She doesn't know how much life she's got left in her, but this is her second chance, and for the first time in years she's actually looking to the future because she can conceive of one. And at the same time, she's telling herself that this is what hope feels like.

* * *

While Vivienne is gazing on to suburban Harrow as if having only just discovered some blessed ordinariness, Stephen is at his desk in Finsbury Park, compiling a list of people to interview. And the first name on the list is Mr Eliot.

He's never met a genius before, mostly because he doesn't believe in them, any more than he believes in God. In his experience there are only people who work hard, have occasional inspired moments, ride their share of luck (because no one gets anywhere without luck) and get results. He glances at the pamphlet, *East Coker*, and the collected poems of Mr Eliot on his desk. He must have read some of the poems in an anthology, maybe one of his mother's, because he's never owned the collected poems before. He picks the book up, flicking through it. Genius, eh? We'll see about that.

Also on his list is Mrs Eliot's brother, Maurice. And this friend of Mrs Eliot's, Miss Purdon. Louise. The chemist. Works close to the asylum. As well as this odd bunch, the Lunacy Law Reform Society. He smiles; they sound like something out of Gilbert and Sullivan. Not that he likes Gilbert and Sullivan, but their name seems made for musical comedy. He can just hear it. But what they do isn't comical, or even musical. They break the law. Simple as that.

While he's contemplating this, his boss walks past and drops a set of car keys on his desk.

'It's the black Humber in the street.'

Stephen looks at them, grinning inside, then at his boss. 'Petrol, sir?'

'Show them this,' his boss says, passing a form to him. He notes the book in Stephen's hand and adds, 'Mr Eliot is speaking at the London Library sometime soonish.'

'Ah.'

'Might be an idea to drop in.'

With that his boss is gone. Stephen watches the Friday afternoon sun dim through the office windows, then picks up the phone and dials. A cheery female voice answers.

'Faber and Faber.'

'Afternoon. I'm Detective Sergeant Minter, Finsbury Park.'

The woman's tone changes immediately. 'Oh, how may I help you?'

'I'd like to make a time to interview Mr Eliot. He works there, correct?'

'Correct. But he's a very busy man.'

'This is not a request. I'm investigating the disappearance of Mrs Eliot from Northumberland House on Wednesday.'

'Oh dear, I didn't know.'

'Mr Eliot has been informed. It's probably too late today; shall we say Monday morning?'

'Mr Eliot works Wednesday to Friday. He's in the country the rest of the time.'

'Well, Wednesday morning. Shall we say nine?'

'Mr Eliot doesn't start until ten.'

'Then ten it is. Thank you, Miss …?'

'Delaney.'

'Thank you, Miss Delaney.'

'You're welcome.'

He hangs up the phone, opens his notepad to a fresh page and begins compiling a list of questions. The day has slipped into mellow twilight by the time he's finished. He pockets his pad, picks up his old army kitbag and heads for the door, tossing the car keys up and down in his hand with a smile, relishing the uncommon luxury of driving back to his bedsit in Stepney.

* * *

In her room Vivienne pours herself another whisky, enjoying the theatre of the street – freedom, she tells herself, never having tasted so good – and places another cigarette into her tortoiseshell holder. Downstairs, George is learning lines for an amateur production; Marjorie is testing him.

Louise Purdon locks the chemist-shop door behind her and strolls home, keeping a wary eye on things around her, half expecting the police to jump out at her any moment. At the same time smiling at the very thought of what they've done.

It worked, she tells herself, it actually worked. Now comes the difficult bit.

Stephen, driving slowly across town, watches the Friday night crowds. Women, here and there, alone or in pairs, quiet or in song, bye and bye, catching his eye. His fox is out there, blending with the throng, keeping low along some lonely park wall, or gone to ground, waiting for night to fall.

WEEK TWO

Early August, 1940

5.

The Weekly Briefing

No pain. No nerves. No waking in the mornings and asking herself how she felt. For a while, when Tom first floated up the river on his punt and into her life – or she up the river and into his – the pain went, the tyranny of the body was toppled. Fell like the statue of a king or a tyrant in some revolutionary square. Brought down, not by some surging mob, but by the accident of falling in love.

Vivienne is standing in a bookshop in Harrow on the Hill, holding one of those green pamphlets that take up much of the window. *East Coker*. Tom's poem. She still finds it odd that he writes things without her being there. Not right, somehow. Writes without passing it over to her to read, as he always did – for however low they may have sunk, however dark the nightmare, however degrading the argument, he always passed his work to her to read. When everything that had brought them together was gone, and almost in an instant, that was the one thing that stayed true through it all and united them. Oh, they may have nearly destroyed each other as human beings, but between them they created T.S. Eliot.

Tom was simply Tom that first day when he stepped off the punt in Oxford and stared at her as she babbled to him over a ragtime tune coming from a gramophone. Unable to take his eyes off her, as if he'd never met anyone quite like her before. And he probably hadn't. But it was equally true that she'd never met anyone quite like him. Transatlantic something or other, they called it. But for all that, Tom was simply Tom that day, hovering on the brink of promise. And it's impossible not to imagine, looking back, that when she impulsively reached out for his hand that day, and he, in a trance, gave it to her, that he was not also handing over his potential. Placing it in her care.

The Tom she met may have signed his poems 'T.S. Eliot', but he hadn't yet grown into the name. He needed shoving, and she shoved with all her might. Now, looking back, there's a large part of her that wishes she hadn't shoved so hard. For in all that shoving and to-ing and fro-ing, they lost each other. He lost the Giaconda smile that so entranced her, and she the sparkle in her eyes. Between them they made T.S. Eliot, but they lost the prize.

She buys the poem and leaves the shop, pausing briefly at the window, and dwelling on the dignified public figure staring out at her, trying to find some trace of her Tom in the portrait. But all she sees is this creation that everybody now accepts as true. The real Tom, *her* Tom, long since shoved out of existence.

In a small park opposite the bookshop she sits on a bench, staring at the pamphlet. East Coker. She's never been there but she feels as if she has. He talked about the place often enough, about that ghostly line of Eliots that left their village for the dark, godless, heathen forests of the New World. So when she opens the pamphlet to read the poem, she reads about a place she has never seen, but somehow knows.

When she's finished, and it doesn't take long, she tucks it into her shopping bag, registering the vague response that she may grow to like it more. But at the moment, it strikes her as being a bit on the pompous side. The sort of thing you write when the spark has gone out of you and all you're left with is the craft. The sort of stuff you might write when you believe your own image, when the creation forgets that he *is* a creation.

She smiles. He hadn't completely lost his accent when she met him. The faint shadow of a Missouri drawl, and the Boston twang was still there. She gazes out over the park, music from an antique gramophone coming out of the past, drifting across the lawns to her, crackling in the air, as she once again floats up the river of her youth towards her future – her future, complete in every detail, already there and just waiting to be lived. That's the thing about a life: once it's lived it's impossible to conceive of it any other way.

She is still mulling over Tom's poem, intrigued by the fact that they have both arrived at the same place, independent of each other. Or, rather, the same moment: she's now looking towards a new life; Tom too. Both of them, their old worlds giving way to the new. Two travellers arriving at the same spot from different directions.

There's something almost satisfying in this, she decides, as she looks around and sees Louise approaching, smiling, a bounce in her step. Ageless. Her friend will, Vivienne is sure, have a bounce in her step when she is old. For herself, Vivienne is sure she will never know old age. She is not one of those who are born to grow old. And it's not just that all those years of struggle and pain and waging war with life have drained her of something, some life force. Still, however short or long, Vivienne can imagine a future now. Something she's not been able to imagine for a long time. And as she thinks back over the wreckage of the years, she can't help but feel the sad waste of it all. That a whole life, *her* life, the only one she'll ever have, has led to this bench and this place in time.

'Afternoon, Vivie,' Louise says, standing in front of her.

'Louie,' Vivienne says, patting a place on the bench beside her, 'sit down.'

Louise sits, then looks Vivienne up and down. 'How are you?'

'How do I look?'

'You look … well.'

'Well-*ish*,' Vivienne says. 'Not sure I've ever done well.'

'Let's settle for well-ish.'

They smile at each other. Planes fly overhead, a bus passes, a baby cries.

'A policeman's been asking questions.'

Vivienne watches the baby being lifted from the pram by its mother, then turns back to Louise.

'What sort of questions?'

'A lot of them. Who visits Mrs Eliot? Who are her friends? Who saw her last? How would you describe Mrs Eliot ... lots of them.'

'What sort of policeman?'

'A young detective sergeant.' Louise pauses a moment. 'He's got your diaries. And a couple of photographs.'

'I should have burnt those diaries ages ago.' Vivienne eyes Louise. 'Why on earth would he be interested in them?'

'I have no idea. He stayed quite a while at Northumberland House and walked away with a list of names.' Louise pauses. 'I'm on it. So you see, we have to be careful.' A quick raising of the eyebrows. 'He's got a limp.'

'How do you know all this?'

Louise rubs her nose. 'I've got someone on the inside.'

'Who? Tell me.'

'You don't need to know.'

'Why not?'

'That's how it works.'

That's how it works ... Mummy listens to Daddy, Vivie listens to Mummy, Maurice ... She eyes Louise, once again seeing her friend as that ageless girl guide explaining the rules of a game they're playing. 'Are you enjoying this?'

Louise dwells on the question, toying with her bracelet. 'Well, as a matter of fact–'

'You are!'

'Don't tell me you're not.'

Vivienne straightens up, scanning the park, mother and baby gone. 'Well, as a matter of fact ...'

Louise grins, then adds, 'Just don't enjoy it too much.'

'Why not?'

'That's how people make mistakes.' It's said with a mixture of the affectionate and the cautionary. 'He's a detective sergeant after all.'

'No plod.'

'No. It means they're serious.'

'Wonder why.'

'You *are* Mrs T.S. Eliot.'

'Mad wife on the loose.' She stares up at the open, blue sky, more or less speaking to herself. 'I frighten them. How odd.'

Louise stands. 'I've got to go. I'll call during the week.'

Then she is gone and Vivienne is alone in the late afternoon, summer shadows long across the paths and lawn. And for the first time since leaving the home, she *feels* alone. Lonely, really. And just a little bit frightened. For the truth is, she has begun to hope. A dangerous thing. She couldn't bear to have her hopes dashed again. She glances at the poem in her hands. *East Coker*. Old lives, new lives. A second chance. And it's as though she's only just realised how much she wants it.

6.

The Detective as Critic

Stephen is making a list of words. Mr Eliot's words. It's the way he reads a case report. He makes a list of the key words. Always has. And, for better or for worse, he's spending the evening reading Mr Eliot's collected poems the same way. Preparation for his meeting with Mr Eliot tomorrow morning.

It's quite a list he's compiling. He's not sure he understands the poems, but this doesn't concern him. It's the words on the list that interest him. The casual mention of Midwestern-cum-continental Semites. Casual as they come, like talking about the weather or seeing a spot on your trousers. The word 'Jew' crops up too, not a lot, but enough. And the words that surround it on the page, about vermin and grubby trade deals suggest the Jew is the lowest of the low. Less than a rat.

One of those Jews, who has a name like something out of a tawdry music hall, spends the poem with a cigar stuck in his mouth, presumably belching foul smoke wherever he goes. His knees are weak, his hands stretched out in an imploring gesture as if saying, 'What can *I* do?' as he proceeds. Bit of an ape, really. He floats through a rotting Venice with other shifty types, their guide a Baedeker. And not just shifty, but cheap. The canal he floats through is murky, the prehistoric sludge and this buffoon of a Jew one and the same.

Other terms on the list are just as bad, all his Jews either shady or unshaven, with slapstick names and paper bags of old, dried fruit. Mr Eliot doesn't say 'grubby' fruit, but he doesn't have to. You can almost smell their breath coming off the page. No, the word 'Jew' doesn't sidle across the page all that often, but when it does the words that surround it are the same every time. Slippery, soiled words, with a five o'clock shadow falling across them. And when Stephen closes the book on these particular poems, he walks away feeling distinctly soiled.

Then there are the words women come draped in when they pad across Mr Eliot's poems on flat, graceless feet, their breasts spilling over the page and their smells coming off it. Men are not spared either: they're old, with decayed, dribbling mouths or agile apes lunging into print.

Everything grubby. Unclean. Rotting. Stephen feels the need to wash his hands after putting the book down. And it's not just the crouching, hunched Jews that stay with him; there's something else one of these screwball characters says – and they all seem to be screwballs – that any man, sometime in his life, has some deep, swampy drive to bump some girl off.

A kind of lingering nastiness hangs about the pages. Snootiness too. There's the pub full of cockney voices. Everybody with names like they'd just crawled out of *Oliver*

Twist or somethink. All talking about teeth and abortions. Reading it feels like listening to someone giving evidence or making a statement, and knowing straightaway that they're lying. Or don't know what they're talking about. Something in the pages doesn't ring true. You get a nose for liars and pretenders. Stephen grew up in the East End. Sometimes he thinks it truer to say he survived the East End. He knows a few things about cockneys and Mr Eliot's cockneys are cartoons.

He walks into his kitchen, in his bed-sit in Stepney, the sort that people in Mr Eliot's poems live in, dwelling on the feeling, the mood that the poems leave you with – it's like the lingering smell of cigarette smoke on your clothes (and Stephen doesn't smoke) after you've been in a pub. The smell of smoke follows you home. That's the way he thinks of Mr Eliot's poems: they leave you with a sort of nicotine stench.

He puts the kettle on, spoons tea into the pot, registering the need to go outside and walk in the fresh air, for the wind to blow away that soiled feeling. The word 'Jew' never felt so personal before. It's not like him; he's never really cared. Stephen Minter has always been just Stephen Minter, neither Jew nor gentile. Jews, gentiles – they were all just people. He's never thought about it much before, never had to, for his parents hardly ever went to synagogue and never really talked much about family history, but he is now. Somewhere back in the family history, grandparents or further back, there were observant Jews. Though not for a while now. So his reaction comes as a surprise, but the word 'Jew', in Mr Eliot's hands, comes with an invisible sneer. And puzzling as it may be, Stephen takes it personally.

All of which makes the next morning's appointment with Mr Eliot an unpleasant prospect. But he's also curious. Just as he's getting a feeling for Mrs Eliot, he's also getting a feeling for Mr Eliot, and he's not sure he likes what he feels, his thoughts and feelings mingling uneasily as steam rises and he inhales the smell of freshly made tea.

He turns the radio on and laughter immediately fills the bed-sit. A comedy. He sits, vaguely taking in the program while looking over the room: cricket trophies on the mantelpiece; a team photograph from before the war; yesterday's newspaper, in front of a family snapshot – Stephen with his parents before they moved down to the coast. A safe distance from London if the bombs ever fall – as they will. He lingers on the shot. His parents. Good people who never ask too much of life, just security and a bit of fun to go on with. Just the sort of people that Mr Eliot looks down on. Laughter erupts from the radio again, but he's not really listening.

There are books on a shelf – cricket tales, detective stories he read when he was young, and novels. Quite a range. He's a reader, always has been, something he got from his mother. There's a novel by one of the new writers, Graham Greene, about a small-time crim called Pinkie. It was a present from a girl before the war, a farewell present. She wrote something inside, signed it 'with fondness'. And 'gratitude'. Fondness wasn't quite what he was looking for. Nor gratitude. He thought he was in love. Even told her so. Not that he had the faintest idea what love was, for when he looks back on himself he seems impossibly young in a way he's not now. She stared at him for some time, then said she was terribly fond of him, but that was all. That was when she bought the book. Odd choice. But she knew he liked Greene, this new voice on the scene. And love? He still doesn't know what it is. How do you know these things? It's easy to kid yourself, convince yourself, tell yourself that this must be it. Or *that* was it. If he was to bump into her again, what would he think now? All he knows for sure is that he was an innocent then. Some of his old school friends were married at twenty. May even have children now. Love, marriage, children. It's still something other people do. All the same, the innocent he was then was blown away by Lillehammer. A sort of innocence that he sometimes misses, like childhood, but not one he wants back.

And while from time to time he might like the idea of having someone else in his life, he's also content with his own company. Something that comes from being an only child? Perhaps. Maybe it's just the way some people fall to Earth. Or in the case of Mr Eliot, the way some people fall to the wrong earth.

He thinks of telephoning his mother and asking what she makes of Mr Eliot's poems. How does she take them? The same way he does? For she has read him; he remembers seeing the poems in the house. But it's late. He'll call tomorrow, after he's spoken to the man. He'll call tomorrow, and they'll talk: about Mr Eliot, how they are, and that constant unease his parents feel about being tucked away in the country. Always feeling one step away from being locked up. Just for being Austrians. Aliens. It's *their* fear he always tells himself, not something real. Haven't they always been safe here? At home?

Stephen downs his tea, switches the radio off and makes his way to the bathroom, lifts his toothbrush from a cup and slowly, thoughtfully, cleans his teeth, spits into the basin and turns for bed. Ten o'clock. The comedy hour will be over. Transmission ceased.

He's left his list of words on the kitchen table, but as he slides into bed, in the black darkness, he's mulling over them.

* * *

Russell Square is green. Almost happy. But quiet. A few workers sitting in the morning sun. Some nannies and babies in prams. No children. All gone to the country. The square, like the streets that once rang with young voices, strangely quiet. No sounds of games. Of squabbles, or laughter. Dreamy. Doesn't look quite real. But it's real all right. A new reality that everyone's still adjusting to.

Stephen turns away from the green square and walks towards a building on a corner of the park. A publishing house. Mr Eliot's. As he approaches the doorway the words in the poems and that soiled feeling comes back to him, and he registers the twin sensations of curiosity and distaste as he steps through the door.

Inside, he puts a face to the pleasant voice on the telephone when he made his appointment. Miss Delaney. Secretary. Younger than he imagined. Not what he pictured, and for a moment he forgets that lingering sense of distaste.

'Detective Sergeant.' It is not so much a question as a deduction. 'You're right on time.'

'I'm very punctual.'

'So is Mr Eliot,' she says, voice friendly, looking over her spectacles. And smiling, but not just a professional smile, a real one. 'I'll take you up.'

As they walk to the stairs, she turns to him, noting the limp. 'He's on the top floor. No lift, I'm afraid.'

'I'm fine.'

They climb the stairs in silence, and when they reach Eliot's door she says, 'Here we are, the eagle's nest. Only don't tell him I said that.'

'Said what?' he says, deadpan.

There's a faint smile on her lips as she knocks on the door and a woman appears, face stern as though something of great importance has been interrupted. She's young too, fresh faced. But she's an old kind of young woman. Bit on the plump side. Looks as though she's no stranger to a hockey field. She dismisses Miss Delaney with a nod, then turns to Stephen.

'He has a very busy day. I hope this won't take long.'

Stephen shrugs, as if to say: as long as it needs to. She ushers him in and a three-piece-suited, late middle-aged man, looking more like a banker than a poet, turns towards him from a desk laden with books and paperwork, and nods gravely, spectacles perched on the end of his nose.

But as much as he may look like a banker or choose to present himself as one, he has an air of importance that could be intimidating, an air that suggests that the likes of Stephen rarely command his time. That it is only because Stephen is the law that he is permitted in this office at all.

And from the moment he enters the office, Stephen is also aware of the strong smell of cigarettes. Not just the morning's butts, but years of cigarette smoke soaked into the walls. What is more, the room smells of foreign cigarettes, like the smell of French railway stations that he noticed on the one and only trip he ever took to Paris. And Mr Eliot himself, he doesn't look well. He gazes at Stephen as if upon an intrusion, while the old young woman who seems to be his personal secretary looks at Mr Eliot – admiringly, protectively.

'If you don't mind, Detective Sergeant, may we begin? We have much work to do today,' Mr Eliot says, his words and manner measured.

'It's about your wife. Mrs Eliot disappeared from Northumberland House almost a week ago.'

'Yes.' Mr Eliot nods, eyes black as a crow, giving nothing away. Stephen may as well have informed him that the government of some tiny, distant republic had fallen. Or a sparrow from the sky. 'What do you know?'

'So far, not much. That's why I'm here.'

'Well, I'm afraid I won't be able to help you much. Unfortunately.' Mr Eliot pauses, and, while he arranges his thoughts, Stephen contemplates the bloodless nature of the 'unfortunately'. 'We've had practically nothing to do with each other since the separation. I wouldn't be giving away any secrets if I said it was a very difficult separation.' The last three words are spoken carefully, every syllable drawn out, emphasising the point. 'This ... disappearance is very troubling. For everybody.'

Again, Stephen can't help but notice that the 'troubling' is as bloodless as the 'unfortunately'.

'She's very fragile, and these are difficult times.'

Mr Eliot's voice is clipped and precise, as if, it seems to Stephen, he's a well-trained actor doing a very good imitation of an Englishman. But he has never heard an Englishman speak quite like this; in fact, he's never heard anybody sound like this at all. Where on earth do you get a voice like that? Stephen knows a few things about accents because he spent much of his school years trying to sound like a proper Englishman – not Austrian, and not like the cockneys he grew up with – but the cockney inevitably got in, and the faint shadow of the Austrian is always there. He wanted to sound like his favourite actors, and spent hours and hours sitting in the darkness of the local cinema mouthing their words. In the end he got it half right.

But Mr Eliot, he's almost believable. The face like a mask, the voice like a foreigner's idea of how an Englishman sounds.

The whole thing an act, a sort of performance. But a very clever one. Almost convincing. Stephen's got to hand it to him, he almost gets away with it. It even gives him the creeps a bit, as if Mr Eliot were his own creator and has invented himself. The whole thing an act that gets him through days like this, Stephen imagines. One that keeps the world at arm's length. For somewhere deep beneath the mask of Mr Eliot, there is surely another one. And perhaps another beneath that. For Mr Eliot gives Stephen the immediate impression of not just being one actor, but a troupe of actors. A man who invites a number of comparisons, for as he contemplates this, Stephen's also wondering if, after peeling back the layers, there would be any core to this onion.

And the age. Another act. In his poem, this pamphlet that is in all the shops, he talks like an old man. But as haggard and pasty and unhealthy as his face may appear, he's not old. All the same, he seems to have adopted the voice of an old man to the point that he believes his own act.

'When you say "fragile", what do you mean? Mind? Body?'

'Both. Always has been. But in many ways not weak at all. Quite tenacious.'

His secretary looks on, compassion, concern and, if Stephen isn't mistaken, a touch of hero worship in her eyes … maybe something more. There are photographs on the wall behind her, one of a man with a cigar sticking out of his mouth. Familiar face. But Stephen can't place it.

'Would you say she was violent, Mr Eliot? Capable of a violent act?'

'No, definitely not. She was known in the family as a bit of a spitfire. But not violent.'

'Temper?'

'Tantrums.'

Stephen pauses for a moment, weighing things up and staring at the gent with a cigar. Then it hits him. Of course, Groucho Marx. A Jew with a cigar stuck in his mouth. Stephen briefly wonders what he's doing up there on the office wall, then returns to Mr Eliot.

'Do you remember where you were when she went missing?'

Here Mr Eliot turns to his secretary.

'Virginia keeps a record of my appointments.'

She asks for the date, flicks through the appointments book, then looks up. 'Shamley Green.'

'I've not heard of it. What is Shamley Green?'

'It's a village. Tiny.'

'You went there by yourself?'

Here the secretary raises her eyebrows and Mr Eliot looks at Stephen, just short of calling the question impertinent. 'I don't see what business that is of yours.'

There it is again, the suggestion that the likes of Stephen rarely take up the time of the likes of Mr Eliot. And for a moment, Stephen is thrown. Tossed, even a bit intimidated. 'It all 'elps, Mr Eliot.'

It is a very rare thing that Stephen drops his 'h's. But it happens. Every now and then something gives way, as it did just then, and the cockney in him spills out of his mouth. For a moment he's considering the possibility that in this matter of accents, at least, he and Mr Eliot might not be so different after all. But what he noticed most was the way Mr Eliot winced when he dropped the unfortunate 'h'. Almost as if he'd been stung. And there's something satisfying about it, like prodding the tightly curled-up ball of some prickly creature and getting a reaction. One of his unfortunate 'h's may well be dropped again.

'I live there four days a week, at the house of an old friend and her sister – if you must know,' Mr Eliot says reluctantly. 'I come up to London for work and fire-watching. Why do you need to know all this?'

'She had help, Mr Eliot.'

'It certainly wasn't me.' It is said in a way that makes it absolutely clear that Mr Eliot would be the last person to help his wife get out.

'No, I see that.'

'Who then?'

'That's the question. Who might have? Any ideas?'

Mr Eliot slowly shakes his head. 'Not really.' He pauses. 'She had a good friend, a Miss Louise Purdon. A chemist, I think. She was very supportive of Vivienne, but I doubt she'd do anything like that. I don't even know if they still see each other, if she visits.'

'She does. Quite regular. A nurse at Northumberland House mentioned her.'

At this point the secretary breaks in. 'I have to remind you that we have a very busy day. Mr Eliot has to cram a week's work into a few days.'

Stephen nods. 'Of course,' then turns to Mr Eliot. 'When did you separate from your wife?'

'Seven years ago.'

'And she was committed three years ago?'

'Yes.'

Again his eyes give nothing away, these the concerns of someone else in another life.

'How often did you visit her?' Stephen knows the answer, but he wants to hear it from Mr Eliot.

'I didn't.'

'Never?'

'No.'

'Why is that?'

The secretary sighs; Mr Eliot's face assumes the hint of a grimace. 'Her doctors strongly advised me not to. That it would do more harm than good.' He pauses. 'You have to understand she never got over the separation. Never accepted it. Always imagined that one day I'd come back. Visiting, I was assured, would only be cruel.'

And you, Mr Eliot, Stephen can't help but conclude, you got over it all too easily. Is that not so? All the same, it is the first vaguely personal thing he's said.

Mr Eliot continues. 'Do you know where she might be?'

Stephen shakes his head, noting a touch of concern in Mr Eliot's voice, but concern for whom or what he's not sure. 'No.' Stephen pauses, grave, then continues. 'Let me ask you, Mr Eliot, is she likely to do herself any harm? Do you think it's possible that Mrs Eliot might do something, well ...'

Here Mr Eliot stares at him, eyes wide, shocked, as though he's been physically struck. As though he's never thought of this. And whether right or wrong, Stephen's instincts tell him that it is not concern for Mrs Eliot behind the shock, but guilt. No, he's not concerned for her, but for himself, and the thought of having to go through life with guilt if his wife's body, one of these mornings, afternoons or evenings, washes up on the banks of the river.

His secretary, with an air of finality, breaks in again. 'Detective Sergeant ...'

'Yes,' Stephen says, rising from his chair.

Mr Eliot watches him, face still shocked at the thought of Mrs Eliot coming to a sudden end. And a grisly one. 'You'll keep me informed?'

'I will. Just one more thing. Do you know anything about a group calling itself the Lunacy Law Reform Society?'

'I've never heard of them. What do they do?'

'They break the law. They smuggle people out of places like Northumberland House. Apparently, there's an old law that says if someone can prove they can live out in the world for thirty days, they're not mad anymore. And they go free. If the court says so.'

'Ah,' Mr Eliot murmurs, as though this too were a possibility he'd never considered. And not one he welcomes.

'Detective Sergeant!' The secretary almost stamps as she speaks, while Mr Eliot looks down at the floor.

She escorts Stephen to the door. In the doorway, he turns round to Mr Eliot. 'Thank you for your 'elp, sir.'

Again the wince, the satisfying feeling of prodding a prickly creature. He makes his way down the flights of stairs to the entrance of the building, passing a grim-faced bald man who looks him up and down without greeting.

'All done then?'

Miss Delaney is distinctly out of place in the building. She smiles, gives the impression of being happy in a place that seems to have either outlawed happiness or looks down on it as an inferior way of being.

'For now,' he says, his mood lightening.

'We might be seeing you again?'

'May do.'

'Well then, we'll still be here. We've never had a detective in before.'

It is at this point that the man he passed on the stairs, and whom he now assumes to be the boss, enters the reception area.

'You are?' he says to Stephen.

'My name's Minter. I'm a policeman.'

For a moment the man is puzzled, then Miss Delaney speaks. 'The detective sergeant had a ten o'clock appointment with Mr Eliot, Mr Faber. About Mrs Eliot.'

'Oh, and you're finished?'

'Yes–'

'Good.'

'For the moment.'

The man drops papers on Miss Delaney's desk. 'Type these up, would you?'

Stephen watches him leave, then turns to Miss Delaney. 'Cheery soul.'

'He has a lot on his mind. They all have. They're not like us, you know,' she says, a faint but definite hint of irony in her voice. Even a playfulness.

'I can see that,' he says, lingering in silence a moment, rightly or wrongly sensing a certain collusion. 'Well, bye then.'

'Nice to meet you, Detective.'

Stephen looks at her, again wondering what she's doing in this place. 'And you too.'

'Don't leave town,' she says, a brief smile passing across her face as she rolls foolscap into the typewriter.

'That's my line,' he says, returning the smile.

'Is there anything else?' she asks, amused, eyes bright.

'There could be.'

'Well, you know where to find us.'

The conversation is left dangling. He nods farewell, she returns the nod, then he slowly swings round to face the door, a puzzled frown on his face as he leaves, as if asking himself – is this what I think it is? Have we just been … flirting?

Russell Square is still green. The sun is still shining. Green park, bright sun. There all the time. But the unnatural silence and that odd sense of unreality hangs over everything, as if he's walking through a dream. And everybody with small boxes slung over their shoulders.

It's good to be stepping into the sunshine, taking in the roses and shrubs, a breeze blowing away the mask of Mr Eliot's face, the sunken black eyes, the heavy smell of cigarette smoke, both in the air and seemingly having seeped into the walls, books and papers.

He walks through the gardens, the limp that will always be there slowing him down. She's well rid of him, Mrs Eliot. That's his immediate reaction. And one, he feels, that is unlikely to change. A story is gradually taking shape. There is much he doesn't yet know about how it will unfold, but he feels sure of this.

When he reaches his car he smiles faintly at having prodded the prickly curled-up ball of the great man and getting a reaction. Mr Eliot, he imagines, is one of those who hide in plain sight behind the three-piece suit of the average businessman, all the time being a troupe of actors, an onion, and a prickly creature rolled up into a ball, hoping nobody notices.

He's also puzzling over Miss Delaney, the odd one out, wondering what it's like when Miss Delaney becomes Emily or

Eva or whatever her name is, suspecting that it could be quite a pleasant experience to be there when she does. Were they really flirting, or was it just him? Whatever the case may be, he takes with him, as he drives back to his office, that lingering feeling of having made a real connection with another human being. A rare feeling, indeed.

7.

Hysteria

'Will the gentleman and the lady be having tea in the garden?'

The waiter is elderly, bald, his hands trembling as he spreads a pink tablecloth over the small cast-iron table. The laughter began innocently. Some harmless joke about a mutual friend. Then the waiter appeared and stood obediently by until they stopped laughing. But they didn't. He stood, fiddling with the pink tablecloth, face halfway between a smile and exasperation. So he stood; so they laughed. 'Will the gentleman and the lady ...'

That was when everything slipped from their control and the laughter ran away from them. Like a bad case of hiccups that threatened to be fatal. Their chests aching, their throats bruised. They were rendered speechless. She tried to nod to the waiter, to say yes, the lady and gentleman will ... But she was like a doll on a string in the hands of some unseen manipulator, and Tom like a jack-in-a-box, hunched in stifled silence one second, springing into uncontrollable laughter the next. Both of them beyond reach.

So the waiter took control and started to lay the pink tablecloth out, smoothing it with trembling fingers. He left them and returned with plates and napkins. All around them Oxford in the spring, the river in front of them drifting through the afternoon, punts here and there, diners glancing, sometimes staring at them. And all the while this demonic laughter seized them. Shelled their sanity, blowing it away, Tom, at one point, concentrating intently on the shaking of her breasts as if that might steady him, and retrieve something from the afternoon, but it only set them off again. They were a spectacle. The afternoon in fragments. Nothing serious in the world. Everything a hoot. All attempts at decorum shot to pieces. They must either go or gather themselves and stay, but they lacked the will and the strength for either.

Then the waiter was in front of them again, holding a tray of tea, cups and cakes, asking once more if the lady and gentleman ... That was when Tom – and it seemed a perfectly splendid thing to do at the time – started barking like a dog. Ruff, ruff, he went. And why not? They were beyond words. She knew exactly what he meant. And what a bark! Utterly splendid. And perfectly understandable. With that, the waiter left the tray on the table and strode away from them as if from some malevolence assuming human form for a few anarchic hours.

Slowly, the laughter died down, her breasts stopped shaking and they no longer had to clutch their sides in pained rapture. Tom poured tea, they bit into cakes, all the time staring at each other silently, as if asking: who *were* those people? And all around them Oxford in the spring, people getting on with afternoon tea as if nothing had happened.

How long had they known each other? Hours? It didn't matter, they both recognised each other immediately. Twin spirits. Here, she beamed, aren't I the very thing you've been looking for, and aren't you the very thing I have travelled all this way to meet?

And hadn't they just sealed the matter in the only way possible? Dispensing with social niceties and manners, for manners are for strangers. That world of social niceties belonged to other people, lesser ones – they were beyond it. Did they not go straight to the heart of things? The dreadful daring of surrendering to some anarchic, elemental force from which there was no coming back, while – unbeknown to Tom and Viv at the time – the gods looked on, laughing even louder than them.

Vivienne lies in her bed, watching the dawn rise over Harrow on the Hill. She has pulled the blackout curtains back, and from her bed observes the changing colour of the sky. The gods were always there, always laughing, only she and Tom never heard them. Only themselves. Ruff, ruff, he went. Another age, another war. But all the same war really, just different uniforms. And weren't they like all fated lovers down through the ages, doomed to end in lament? Everything a re-enactment of what had gone before and will come after: the lovers, the laughter, the story – unchanging through changing styles and changing times. He, some transatlantic Romeo. She, Juliet in ragtime. Even now, she can hear the crash of the cymbals signalling the doomed convergence. Bury meets Missouri; Missouri, Bury. And all the time the gods laughed through them, inhabited them, possessed them, then when their sport was done, strode away, laughing louder still.

If they'd had any sense they both would have walked away that afternoon too. If they'd had any sense they would have just had a torrid affair, and when they were spent, all passion drained from them, gone their separate ways. No harm. No damage. But they didn't, they'd given up all sense. They dived in. Took the chance of their lives and took the leap of faith. Straightaway before they could have second thoughts. The dreadful daring of just diving in. Fly or fall. They never stood a chance. She sees that now; Tom saw it all too soon. It was over before it had barely begun.

The house is silent. No one else has yet stirred. A good time for thinking, or a bad one. Depending on the thoughts. There are some days and nights from the past that are the last things she wants to recall – and, of course, they're the first things that spring to mind.

Eastbourne. Honeymoon. Tom in a chair with his head in his hands, like some Notre Dame gargoyle, blood on the marriage bed. But not virgin's blood because she wasn't one. Tom was. The blood was auntie, who always came at the wrong time, and often in a flood.

This was where the dive ended, where the leap landed. There was Tom, sailing towards the grown-up life where couples made love and fretted over money. Twenty-seven years of expectation. The act itself about to disclose its mystery. Man, woman, conjunction. Twenty-seven years, and all over in a second or two. And she'll never forget the look in his eyes just before he buried his face in his hands, staring at her as if upon a stranger, or as if looking at her for the first time and discovering a different woman altogether and pronouncing himself fortune's fool. Or rather, seeing the woman who was always there, as apart from the one he *chose* to see. Then he saw the blood on the sheets and the look turned to horror.

Even now, she lives it all again: gathers up the sheets and, at first, implores Tom to speak. To just say something. But he doesn't look up, he doesn't speak. She implores him again, and again there is no reaction. Tom in his pyjamas, turned to stone. Even now, in awful clarity, she sees herself walking past him, the offending sheets gathered in her arms, before she runs the bath and drops them in and returns to the bedroom.

And then her high-pitched scream shatters the silence of the room. A wail to wake the dead. Still he sits, face in hands, saying nothing. Still she screams, until there is a thump on the door from the hallway. Are you all right in there? Yes, yes, she hears Tom saying. Yes, yes. The voice in the hall retreats. Silence again. Her screams exhausted, she dissolves into tears and collapses on the floor in her nightdress. Selfridges. Their finest. Purchased the day before. The day before, in another life. First came the laughter, then the laughter turned to screams, and the screams to silence.

Vivienne, eyes wet, rises and watches the dawn stride over the rooftops of Harrow on the Hill. Old tears, the very same tears shed decades ago, being shed all over again. Heart thumping. To love and be loved. That is all there is. But when he floated up the river and into her life, all innocence and enchantment, he also brought hidden deep inside him this other Tom, this New England Tom, still haunted by devils and witches, that she didn't notice then. Or did she, but chose to ignore it?

'What have we done?' he finally said. And it was spoken in a way that said, this is now our burden. Our cross that we shall have to carry through the years. We succumbed to the devil's laughter. To the devil's dare. To the devil's hysteria. There is no going back and nothing to be done. And it was spoken in a way that said – I thought I loved, but I know now that I never did and never have. I was much deceived and never knew until now. I have deceived myself, I have deceived you. I have no one to blame but myself. And there is nothing to be done but accept it and get on with things. I lusted, but did not love. Now my lust is laid bare, a toothless devil grins, and my love is a sham.

The lights in the shop across the street come on. Morning comes to Harrow on the Hill. The same way it came to that sombre honeymooners' bedroom all those years ago. Ruefully, apologetic, the sun afraid to show its face. The scene that told its own tale, the moment when dreams shattered, when the leapers landed, and a marriage died before it had even begun. Stillborn. The marriage bed sheets soaking in the bath. Romeo hunched with his head in his hands; his Juliet, all tears and screams wrung from her, collapsed in her nightdress on the floor.

The day's first customer steps through the shop door opposite. If anyone was to ask Vivienne what sort of marriage it was, she would say it was a marriage of silence – and screams. Uncontrollable laughter, hysteria and hollow despair. A sentence, not a union – only she couldn't accept it, could never accept that their spectacular leap into life had landed in that wretched place, while Tom accepted it all too soon.

There are sounds of life coming from downstairs. They are preparing for the day. A van passes along the street. A barrage balloon, 'Winston' she's told, hovers in the distance. Yesterday's and today's tears now dried, she sits before the mirror, Polly on her lap, runs a comb through her hair and begins preparing her face.

8.

Miss Purdon's Lies

A small formation of bombers passes overhead, almost like a flight of ducks, either coming from or flying to their feeding grounds. A barrage balloon hovers in the still air, a silver tethered rugby ball glinting in the sun. Stephen shakes his head; he can't believe they do anything. There to reassure people more than anything else. Not that anyone really notices them anymore. Doesn't take long for the absurd to become normal.

The bombers recede and blend into the horizon as he turns and enters the chemist shop. Bottles, bottles everywhere. Glass cabinets, the faint whiff of ether. The shop is hushed, a drugged silence hovering over everything.

A bright-faced middle-aged woman materialises at the counter. 'Can I help you, sir?'

Stephen nods. 'I'm looking for Miss Purdon. I believe she works here.'

'That's me,' she says, the bright face giving way to frowned curiosity. 'Who are you?'

'My name's Minter. I'm a policeman.'

'Oh.'

There is a hint of concern beneath her curiosity, but she gives nothing away. Miss Purdon exudes an air of efficiency. One of those used to taking charge and getting things done. Born unflappable.

'It's about Mrs Eliot.'

'Ah, what about her?'

'You know Mrs Eliot?'

'Yes.'

'She's gone missing from Northumberland House.'

'I heard.'

'How?'

'We supply them with medicine. A nurse told me.'

'And you supplied Mrs Eliot with her medicine?'

'Yes. She used to come in sometimes.'

'How's that? It's an asylum.'

'She'd slip out,' Miss Purdon says, as if it were perfectly obvious. 'The gates aren't always manned.'

'And she'd seize her chance.'

'Yes. Bit of a devil.'

Stephen pauses, taking this in. 'Are you friends?'

Miss Purdon weighs her answer. One of those who preview their thoughts before speaking. 'She's a very lonely woman. She seemed almost alone in the world. Apart from Polly.'

'Who's Polly?'

Miss Purdon smiles. 'Polly isn't a who. Polly is her dog. A silky terrier. Dear thing. The dog was devoted to her. And

Mr Eliot. The dog was their child, I suppose. And when they separated, Polly was like the child caught in between. Sad. So, apart from the dog, she didn't really seem to have anybody close. Everybody turned their backs on her.'

'Everybody?'

'All those so-called friends. They all sided with Mr Eliot, and turned their backs on her. Suddenly she was alone. And lonely. She calls me her friend. And I am happy for her to do so.'

'How long have you known her?'

'A number of years. I took her meals, did some housework. Before the asylum. The place was a mess. She didn't seem to have the will or the strength to do the ordinary things. So I helped out.'

'After Mr Eliot left?'

'Yes.'

'When was the last time you saw her?'

'Some time ago; I can't exactly remember,' she says, poker-faced.

'But not since she escaped?'

'Heavens no, why do you ask?'

'She had help.'

'Getting out, you mean?'

'Yes.'

'Why do you think that?'

Stephen shrugs. 'Believe me, she had to.'

'But I've just explained she was perfectly capable of giving them the slip all by herself. She's done it before.'

Stephen eyes her for a moment. She's poised, impassive. And plausible. But she's lying. Pretty good, but good in the way that a good forgery is.

'How did Mrs Eliot strike you?'

'In what way?'

'Well, did she come across as—'

'Mad? No. She did some mad things. Came in one night in blackshirt uniform. Full fascist outfit. Made it herself. Been out on the town. Made a stir, apparently.'

'Is she a fascist?'

Miss Purdon shakes her head. 'She joined, did telephone work for them in the office, but I think she just wanted some attention. She's lonely. But she's not mad. Sane as anyone. Probably saner than most.' She pauses, eyeing Stephen suspiciously, as if to say: why are you interested in this? Then she adds, wistfully, 'She's been almost serene over the last year or so. Had a sort of stillness about her.' She stares out the window then looks back at Stephen. 'Sane.'

'Sane enough to give them the slip all by herself?'

'Certainly.'

'Enough to arrange some place to go? You see, this is it – where did she disappear to?'

Miss Purdon smiles. 'I'm afraid you'll have to ask her that.'

'You don't have any idea?'

'How could I?'

'You're her friend.'

'I'm happy for her to call me a friend. Even so, we haven't been in contact lately.'

He eyes her again, the conversation becoming a bit of a game. She's a good liar, but not good enough to disguise the fact that she *is* lying.

'Have you heard of the Lunacy Law Reform Society?'

'I've heard of it.'

'Ever have anything to do with it?'

'Never.'

'Ever met anyone who does?'

'No.'

Stephen draws breath. Lies. All of it.

The door opens, a customer enters. Another woman comes to the counter to take her order. Miss Purdon, an air of being pleased with herself, asks, 'Are we nearly finished?'

'Nearly.' He sways slowly from one foot to the other, easing the pain in his knee. 'Let's suppose she had help.'

'All right, let's suppose.'

'Who do you think might have helped her?'

'How on earth would I know?'

'Let's suppose.'

'Certainly not her husband. He never visited. I suspect he'd be happy for her to stay inside forever. Have you spoken to him?'

'Yes.'

There's a faint twinkle in her eyes. 'How did he strike you?'

He ignores the question. 'She has a brother.'

'Maurice. He might have signed her in. Along with the doctors. Maybe he realised it was a mistake and had a fit of guilt. But I doubt he'd be up to something like this. Who knows? You've met him?'

'No.'

Another customer enters. Miss Purdon smiles at her, then turns to Stephen.

'Mr ...'

'Minter.'

'Mr Minter, are we finished?'

'For now.'

'If you don't mind me asking, what is your rank?'

'I'm a detective sergeant.'

In spite of herself, and in spite of already knowing, she looks impressed. But also looks him up and down as if to judge him a little young for such a rank. Either it's the war, or he's smart. Or both. 'Tell me, Detective Sergeant, why is someone like you spending all this time looking for Mrs Eliot?'

'Orders.'

'Things are falling apart–'

'There are those who think that Mrs Eliot isn't just anybody, because Mr Eliot isn't just anybody.'

'And we can't have the great man's mad wife running round on the loose?'

Stephen leaves the question in the air. 'Thank you, Miss Purdon. I may be back.'

Miss Purdon nods as Stephen turns to leave, then busies herself with some paperwork.

Outside, the barrage balloon is still up there in the sky. And the ducks, like the mysterious Mrs Eliot, have flown. But to where, Stephen wonders, gazing upon the expanse of Greater London.

* * *

When Stephen returns to the station, his chief is waiting for him. And from the moment he steps into his superior's office, Stephen knows from the look on his face that something has happened.

'Sit down, Minter.'

Stephen sits.

'Have you heard of Lord …'

He mentions a lord. A famous one. High up in government.

'Yes, sir.'

'His estranged wife shot him last night.'

'Ah.' Stephen's unmoved air suggests he's not sure why he's been hauled into the boss's office to hear this.

'Yes, ah,' his boss says, slightly taken aback by Stephen's casualness. 'In the arm, luckily. His withered one. Doesn't use it anyway. It was point blank. No question, she wanted to kill him. Lousy shot, thank God.' He pauses, gauging Stephen's reaction now. 'He's been discharged from hospital. Still in shock. She's been locked up. Just like your Mrs Eliot should be.'

Stephen allows himself one of those internal smiles that don't show on the lips but light up the brain. When, he wonders, did she become 'his' Mrs Eliot?

'Your Mrs Eliot,' his chief goes on, 'before she was committed, was getting around town with a knife in her handbag.'

'It was a stage knife, sir. I read it in the report.'

'I don't care if it was a stage knife or a machete.'

'I doubt you'd fit a machete in a handbag, sir.'

His chief glares at him. 'This is no joke, Minter.'

'No, sir.'

'No, sir indeed. It's the intent, Minter. Next time it could be real. Or a gun.' He stares at Stephen, letting the point sink in. 'Find her.'

'That's what I'm doing, sir.'

'Minter,' his chief says with a hint of distaste, 'your needle's out there somewhere.'

Just as Stephen never much thought of himself as Jewish – he's neither hidden it nor made a fuss of it – until he read Mr Eliot's poems, he's also realising there are other things he may never have noticed before. Like the hint of distaste in the chief's voice. And, at the same time, he realises that there's a fair bit of it about. More than you might think. And in surprising places.

'Find her! And fast. That's all.'

As Stephen rises, he concludes that somebody is leaning on his chief. And hard. He goes to his office and begins writing up his notes on Miss Purdon.

When he's finished he leans back in his chair, the afternoon sun lighting up the shops and houses opposite, washing them, almost cleansing them. But it's the telephone he's contemplating. And once more he's wondering what it might be like to be there when Miss Delaney becomes Emily or Eva or whatever it is that Miss Delaney calls herself. Whatever happened, she's the one bright thing to emerge from this whole murky business. He also has to admit he's wondering what she knows. Secretaries know a lot. He opens his address book and taps the desk with his fingers.

Then he's dialling the number with no idea what he'll say, at the same time scanning the entertainments in the paper. His eyes hit upon a notice as he hears Miss Delaney's voice.

'Good afternoon, Faber and Faber.'

'Afternoon, Miss Delaney. This is Detective Sergeant Minter.'

'Oh, I'm afraid Mr Eliot isn't in today.'

'Actually,' he says, diving straight in, 'I wasn't calling about Mr Eliot.'

'Oh?'

'I was calling you.'

'Really,' she says, a mixture of surprise and curiosity. 'And why is that? Don't tell me I'm a suspect.'

'They're showing the *Rue Morgue Murders* in Leicester Square.'

There is a slight pause. 'And?'

'I thought you might like to see it.'

There is another, longer pause. 'With you?'

'That's the idea. Of course, if ...'

Silence. He counts: one, two, three ...

'*Rue Morgue Murders.*' She laughs. 'Who could pass that up?'

'That's what I was hoping,' he says, sending a relieved smile down the line. 'Shall I come by the office?'

'Yes.'

'At six?'

'I'll be here.'

'I hope you won't mind going in a police car?'

She laughs again. 'Murder, dead bodies, police car. Bliss. Can I ring the siren?'

'Only if we're late.'

'I think I should warn you I'm always late,' she says slowly, and he can imagine the smile at the other end of the line.

'See you at six.'

'Six, then.'

With that they hang up and Stephen, a quizzical smile on his face, as if asking himself if that really just happened, gazes out over the sunlit shops and houses opposite, the shadows of his chief's voice banished for the moment, that unclean feeling gone, and all because of a simple yes.

Then he returns to his notes. Find her! his chief ordered. Easily said. The expanse of Greater London looking more expansive with every passing day.

* * *

Miss Delaney slips into the front seat of the car, staring up at the top floor of the office as she does.

'He's up there and watching. I can see him at the window. Old Eagle Nose.'

Stephen looks at her, puzzled. 'Mr Eliot?'

'Yes.'

'I thought you said he wasn't in today.'

'I lied,' she says, a smile in her eyes.

He raises his eyebrows. 'Cheeky.'

'I had to. I was told to say that Mr Eliot isn't in today. Sorry, it was either lie or lose my job.'

They pull out from the kerb, the shadow of Mr Eliot at his window, looking down on the square, slowly receding.

'You're a good liar. I should know.'

'You get good at it. It's a sort of house skill. Mrs Eliot was before my time, but everybody lied to her for years. Mr Eliot isn't in today, they'd say, and all the time he would be slipping out the back door. Mrs Eliot standing there with a box of chocolates for Tom, wondering what to do with it. Not sure I could have done that.' She sighs, possibly dwelling on the picture of Mrs Eliot and the chocolates. 'Good to get out of the place. It's like a fortress in there these days. Everyone's on edge.'

'Over Mrs Eliot?'

'They're terrified. The mad woman's out of the attic. They're all in quite a state.'

They pass a small street stall. There are sudden screams. Voices, loud and nasty. You thieving bitch! They both turn to the scene on the footpath. Two women fighting over a package of some kind. The package tears, sugar cascades to the ground and the two women stare at it. One woman falls to her knees, scooping up the precious white granules, the other striding away.

'They're not the only ones on edge,' Stephen says, eyes back on the road.

'What's going to happen if the bombs start falling?'

'Not *if*, when.'

'Poor Mrs Eliot, out there somewhere in this. Whenever I picture her I think of a small bird. A sparrow, perhaps. Not sure why.'

'Sparrows are survivors.'

'They better be.'

'Tell me, Miss Delaney …'

She smiles, breaking in before he can finish whatever the question is. 'Detective Sergeant, we *are* going to the pictures together. We left Miss Delaney back there. It's Brigid sitting here.'

Ah, so that's it. He wouldn't have picked her for a Brigid, but now that he knows she is it's obvious.

'Stephen,' he says, 'at the wheel.'

She nods, smiling. 'I like the sound of that. Some people wind up with the wrong names. Don't you think?'

'I've never thought about it.'

'I have. But you're fine. You look like a Stephen.'

He smiles. 'Pleased to hear it. For what it's worth, you're my first Brigid.'

She leans back in her seat, taking in the scene. 'And you are my first Stephen. Unless we include Stephen Spender. He drops in to the office every now and then.' She turns to Stephen, smiling. 'That doesn't count, does it?'

'No.'

'Besides, he's always Mr Spender anyway. Now, what was the question?'

He laughs. 'Forgotten.'

The early evening traffic is light as they turn into Southampton Row. Shops open, an organ-grinder somewhere. Dreamy streets. People going about their business as if nothing much has changed.

'I like names. I think they matter. If I were a writer I'd spend most of my time thinking about what to call my characters and never get anything written.'

As they pull up at the lights, he turns, looking at her. Fine brown hair, spectacles gone, playful eyes.

'How on earth did you wind up in that place? That's what I was going to ask you.'

'My father went to school with Mr Faber.'

'Ah.'

'School ties,' she says, watching the shadowy mix of soldiers, airmen and civilians making their way home. 'I looked forward to it at first. Chance to meet some famous writers. But that wore off. I don't mind it.' She pauses, stroking the tip of her nose in thought. 'But it's a bit like working in one of those posh gentlemen's clubs. They've got names for each other. Mr Eliot's the possum. I've forgotten what Mr Faber is – the elephant, probably. It's a bit like stepping back into the last century.' She turns to him. 'What time do the murders start?'

'Six thirty.'

She checks her watch. 'Good heavens, we're late.'

He gives her a quick, quizzical glance. 'You can't be serious.'

'Where's the switch?'

'I could lose my job.'

'No, you wouldn't. Where is it?'

'Miss Delaney …'

'Brigid.'

He shakes his head, eyes on the road. 'It's the green thing on my left.'

'Ah,' she says, locating it, eyes lighting up. 'The wonderful green thing.'

Before he has time to say anything more, the car explodes with metallic, high-pitched ringing. More of an alarm bell than a siren. The traffic parts, the road opens up. She leans back in her seat, a sly smile on her face, savouring the moment, the excitement of legally breaking the law, passing cars and vans and people, bells ringing.

'They'll think I've been arrested.'

He grins, staring at her, eyes off the road. So this is what it's like to be there when Miss Delaney becomes Brigid. The car veers to the wrong side for a moment, his eyes swing back to the road as he corrects things.

Amused more than anything, she says, 'Where did you learn to drive?'

'Army. A Beaverette.'

'A what?'

'Armoured car. Reconnaissance.' He grins as he shifts gear. 'Machine gun. Bren.' His grin widens. 'Not your average motor.'

She eyes him silently, the hint of a smile, registering the lad inside the detective sergeant, then calls out above the din, 'You and the army, what happened?'

His grin fades. 'It's a short story. Not so interesting. I'll tell you later. Okay?'

She nods. 'Okay.'

The traffic thickens as they head towards Leicester Square. The daylight lingers and soon they come to a stop, the square a short walk away. He switches the siren off. The sound of ringing subsides. She looks around as if emerging from a delicious dream.

'I'm afraid the picture's going to be a let-down after that.'

'We don't have to go. There's a good pub nearby. So what is it, pictures or pub?'

'Pub,' she says, no hesitation.

As they step out of the car, Stephen, ears still ringing, is wondering what other surprises she's got in her. And as though she's read his thoughts, she says, 'You're wondering what you've got yourself mixed up with, aren't you?'

He shakes his head. 'Not at all.'

She grins. 'Liar.'

The pub windows are taped and already blacked out, but when someone leaves and the door swings open, a honeyed wedge of light beckons from inside. A sort of welcome. They step through the doorway.

When Stephen puts their beers down on the table, they drink and then he leans back in his chair. 'Supposing I was wondering what *have* I got myself mixed up with. What would you say, just supposing I asked?'

She lowers her pint, thoughtful. 'A bit of a posh girl from a bit of a posh school. I liked it, but it was a goldfish bowl. Kept on bumping into the same fish. One day I thought, if I'm not careful, I'll end up marrying one of them. And that would be the end of that. Next thing you know you've got a little fish of your own and she's going to the same school you went to. And then she has a little fish, and so on and so on. Till the end of ...' She dwells a moment on the thought, then shrugs. 'The thought of being twenty and life being settled wasn't what I was looking for. Now, just what I *am* looking for, that's another thing. Let's just say I've found what I *don't* want.' She comes to a stop again, touching the tip of her nose. 'Oh, and my father's a civil servant. High up. And my mother keeps herself busy. That's me. What about you?' She grins. 'Let's get this over with.'

She lifts her beer and sips while looking around the pub. Quiet people. Quiet conversations. A dog on the floor under the next table. Stephen raises his eyebrows a little as if there's nothing much to say.

'I'm the son of Austrian immigrants. Came here in 1930. Father a tailor, mother a high-school English teacher. Couldn't get a job here so she looked after the books when my father opened a shop. Stepney. Where we lived. Where I still live. No posh school. They're in the country now. They wanted to live by the sea, but they're not allowed to. Austrians. Enemy aliens. Their status is under review. Been living here for ten years – it's ridiculous. My mum's petrified they'll be put in a camp. Still, they could be back in Austria. We all could.' He pauses. 'Oh, and we're Jewish.'

She's nodding, taking it in. Taking Stephen in, drawing silent conclusions and he'd love to know what they are.

'You don't talk like Stepney.'

This is something he's noticed: she comes at you from different angles. He likes it. Keeps you on your toes. 'How does Stepney talk?'

'Not sure, but not like you.'

'How do I talk?'

'Like you've had lessons.'

'You *could* say that. But if I have I took lessons from Robert Donat and my academy was the local cinema. Besides, my mother was an English teacher. She's not a snob, but she can't stand cockney, couldn't from the start, and wasn't going to have it in the house.'

'Common?'

He grins. 'Somethin' o' that.'

She has an amused, quizzical look in her eyes. And for the first time he's noticing that she's relatively small and compact. And for all her talk about being posh, that's not what comes across. Something else does, but what?

'You enjoy being a copper?' she asks, breaking into his thoughts.

He's slow to answer, still dwelling on the 'what'. 'Yes and no. Not sure I'm cut out for it, though.'

'I know what you mean. My job was a chance to meet Mr Eliot, but there are times when I wish I hadn't.' She sighs. 'I suspect we're better off just reading a writer's books and not meeting them.' She tilts her head to one side, as if re-appraising the thought. 'They call him the pope of Russell Square.'

He frowns. 'Why?'

'He makes writers the way the pope makes saints. Oh, he's all right, I suppose. Depending on the day.' Here she grins, remembering something. 'I made a typing mistake one day – posh girls don't type, you see – and I said "shit" – they say "shit". Mr Eliot just happened to be there. He didn't say anything, but the look on his face was enough. I'd lowered the tone of the place. A once is *just* tolerable, but it better not happen again sort of look.' She laughs at the memory. 'Mind you, when they all get together – Possum, Elephant and the rest of the zoo – you can bet they say the same things and a lot worse. How did he strike you?'

The pub door swings open and three soldiers walk in, take a table and slump into chairs. Stephen eyes them. Knows the types. Sullen, edgy. Looking for trouble if there's any around. One of them clocks him and eyes his civvies as he goes to the bar. Stephen returns to Brigid.

'Strange thing,' he eventually says, 'I never felt remotely Jewish until I read him.'

She ponders this, as if she's not sure what he means. Then something clicks. 'All those grubby Jews?'

'You noticed too?'

'Not until now,' she says, a slow shaking of her head, disappointed in herself.

Everything she's said until now has been, more or less, playful. But there's nothing playful in the way she says this. And he's aware, properly aware for the first time, that he is completely at ease with her. There are no awkward silences, no wondering what to say next. And she can't be too long out of school, he imagines, but she's somehow older than her years.

'Why didn't you go to university?'

'I did, for a year. Cambridge, of course. Same fish, bigger bowl. Where did you get the leg?'

He stares at her for a moment, as if to say: I'd forgotten about that. And he had. Distraction, as he's found, being the best anaesthetic.

She looks suddenly concerned. 'You don't mind? My asking?'

'No, not at all. Norway.'

'Oh.'

'Nothing more to say, really.'

'No,' she says, genuine sympathy in her eyes.

'I had a walk-on part in a stuff-up. Like I said, a short story.' There is a brief silence. She waits for him to go on. And when he does resume he's aware that he's never really talked about this before. Not something you're supposed to talk about. 'Some blokes are affected more than others. Their nerves get shot, they have nightmares. Can't sleep. I'm one of the lucky ones – I've always been able to stand back. Just get on with things. And nothing stops me sleeping.' She's looking at him, nodding but unconvinced. 'I'm okay, really. I don't need sympathy,' he says.

'I don't doubt that, but you've got it anyway.' She pauses, taking him in, somewhere in her eyes the suggestion that they haven't finished with this. 'So,' she finally says, her tone playful again, 'if you don't want sympathy, what do you want?'

He looks down, frowning at his empty glass. 'Another beer. You?'

She nods and hands her glass over. Stephen rises and as he nears the bar, he nods to the soldiers. 'Evening, gents.'

'What's it to you?' the one who caught his eye says. 'We got mates dying out there while you walk around like there's no war at all. Nice war for some.'

Stephen ignores them, gets the beer, and returns.

'What did he say to you?' Brigid asks, a touch of steel in her voice.

'Nothing.'

'It wasn't nothing.'

'It doesn't matter.' His voice is calm, even reassuring. And then, to change the subject, he says, 'Are you going to stay with your job?'

She looks across at the table, eyeing the soldiers, still not ready to let the matter go. 'Do you get much of that?'

'A bit.'

She nods, as if to say a bit is a bit too much. 'I've already organised to leave.'

'To do what?' he says, focusing on her closely, deciding that he's never met anyone quite like her before. A free spirit, goes her own way. Comes at you from different angles. Quick on her feet. Eyes that don't miss much. If anything.

'I've wanted to do something more for a while. Didn't feel like sitting the war out in Russell Square. Typing up rejection letters.' She smiles. 'Sometimes I think everybody's writing books and nobody's reading them.' She takes a sip of beer. 'It was fine for a time, but I want more than that. So I applied for this … place, and got it.'

'What place?'

A slow shaking of the head. 'Can't say.'

He nods. 'That sort of place.'

'It's new. In the country. I start in two weeks.'

'No point asking where.'

'Not really.' Her face brightens. 'But I'll be coming down to London from time to time.'

'You know where to find me.'

She leans back in her chair, breathing in deeply. 'I feel like I'm finally going to *do* something. You see, you've actually done something ...'

'Took part in a stuff-up.'

'But you *did* something, and you're doing important work now.'

'Chasing Mrs Eliot?' He shakes his head. 'I'm starting to feel quite sorry for her, actually. My boss told me to find her fast. Lord Whatsit's wife shot him last night.'

'I heard. Nasty type. Pity his wife didn't shoot him earlier. Surprised she didn't. They call him the copulator. Mistresses everywhere. Must be at it all the time, except with Lady Whatsit.' She pauses a moment, eyes on some far point of the pub. 'I met him once, a few years ago. Revolting experience. Withered arm like some sort of broken wing, eyes all over you. Yuk.'

Stephen laughs. 'What do all those women see in him?'

There's a half smile on her face, a shadow of contempt. 'They feel sorry for him, and he plays on it. For all it's worth. My father hates him. He wanted to surrender, except he called it peace. He's been hunting with Goering and had a jolly fine time. No, pity his wife didn't shoot him sooner. Bad luck she missed.'

He grins. 'I'll let my chief know.'

'You do that. I don't care who hears.'

He looks down at the table, to their empty glasses.

'One for the road?'

She shakes her head. 'I'll push off.'

'Let me drive you.'

'Thanks, but I'll take the tube.'

'Where to?'

She grins. 'St John's Wood.'

He lifts his eyebrows. 'Nice.'

'Full of the nicest people.'

They rise and head for the door, but when they reach the table with the three soldiers she stops.

'Evening, gents.' They look up, puzzled, sullen and silent. 'You've heard of Norway? Well, my friend left his leg there in case you didn't notice.'

She turns away without waiting to see their reactions and they both step outside. The light is fading, the streets emptying. The houses in blackout.

'I know, you're wondering just who it is you've got mixed up with.'

He smiles, taking in the gleam in her eyes. 'Crossed my mind.'

They stop at the entrance to the station.

'Who knows,' he says, 'next time we might really take in a show.'

'We just might.'

She tilts her head and gives him a quick kiss on the lips. Over before he knows it's begun.

'Can I have that again?'

She shakes her head, smiling. 'Don't think I'm easy just because I rang your siren.'

They both laugh, and with that she makes her way down the station stairs, turning and waving as she goes. He waves back and when she's disappeared he walks to his car. The ease of their talk, that sense of being comfortable with her, of having met someone the likes of whom he's never met before, stays with him on the footpath and throughout his drive home to Stepney. And as he heads east he can't help but think of her stepping out of the tube station into St John's Wood – different worlds, but same city – right now. Just a few miles away. A few days ago there was no Brigid Delaney in his life. And it is, he's suddenly realising, the first time he's let someone into his life since he got back. Lord Whatsit might milk his withered arm for all it's worth, but until now Stephen was never sure if someone liked him or noticed his leg and just felt sorry for him.

Stepney looms. Grimy back-to-backs that haven't had a clean in fifty years. Streets deserted. Except for the local. Streets that look like trouble, and often are. As he steps out of the car, two men in uniform spill out of the pub and make their uncertain way up the street. Stephen turns the key in his front door and closes it all out. Nice war for some. Short war for some. He mounts the stairs, the faint ringing of bells in his ears and a smile that wasn't there the day before.

9.

London Bridge is Falling Down, Falling ...

The city's towers collapse and tumble to the ground. Bridges sink into the river, a bus slides into the murky waters, the driver with a look of mild surprise on his face, the passengers looking out with dull-eyed resignation. This is the way the world ends. This is the way of it. Collapse and fall. Parliament, banks, departmental offices, libraries and church spires become rubble and dust. Trains roll over on their sides and expire. Birds and bats fall to earth, twitching on the ground. Early morning crowds, eyes down, press on to work. Wave after wave. Thunder rumbles across the canyon of the city. The river barges are loosed from their moorings.

One lost soul, through whom the last vestiges of a vanished, perfect life speak – the life of simple faith and fruitful fields and tolling bells calling all to prayer – wanders through the ruins of this civilisation. Picks his way through the rubble, seeking signs of the vanished life, communing with its ghosts. The sky swirls, cinders fall, day becomes night, and the lost soul alights at a window sill where a woman sits, drawing her hair out of its bindings, while staring across the street at the summer spectacle of a pub at closing time.

That's how he saw himself, Tom. Couldn't help but see himself, because he was a lost soul. A lost soul who, brolly in hand and bowler hat just so, picking his way through the rubble, wore that just-landed look to work and back again: the sailor home from the sea, the pilgrim home for dinner. He wore that look in the kitchen, in the sitting room, and at that very moment when he alighted at the window sill, slipped through the window and curled up in his favourite armchair.

Across the street the barman is calling for last orders. The woman sitting at the window sill, drawing her hair out, fingers trembling, speaks, mimicking the pub's drinkers.

'Go on, Effie. 'Ave anovver. Oh Lol, you are a devil. You only live once, Effie. Is that true, Lol? Do you really fink so?' She turns to the silent, seated figure of her husband in the armchair. 'What do they call this street? I've never noticed.'

'Ratty Row.'

She smiles, a brittle smile. 'Yes, that's it. Ratty Row. Perfect.'

She draws her hair out again in jerky movements, humming a ragtime tune, the sounds of the pub wafting up to her. ''Ere, Stell,' she continues, 'take me pay, take all me pay and get yerself some lovely, white new chompers. You're a sight. You know that? You only live once. Oh Lol, you say that like it's already over ...'

She turns to her husband, who sits glum and silent, for a reaction. Barely of this world. Has he even heard? Does he even bother to listen? Does he take anything in or is she wasting her breath? Suddenly, like the storm that's been rumbling all night, she breaks.

'Speak!'

It is an ear-piercing shriek that would have any normal person jumping in their chair. But this is not a normal person. They are not a normal couple.

'Speak! You never say anything. Never!'

She assaults him with question and accusation. One after the other. Again and again. Say something. Why do you say nothing? Why? Is there nothing in your head? No life? No mind? Are you dead? Are *we* dead? But the fortress of her husband remains unmoved, infinitely patient. He stares back from his armchair. Still in his work clothes: suit, tie, handkerchief tucked into his breast pocket. Just so. His eyes staring out from the mask of his face. Hands folded. Silent.

She jumps out of her chair, yelling. Hurling volley after volley of accusation and question, volley after volley bouncing off the fortress walls.

'If you don't say something, if you don't do something, I'll burst! I can't bear this. Nobody can. Speak! Anything. Babble. I don't care. Are you alive or dead? Is there any life left in you? Say something, for God's sake!'

Eyes still, gazing at her as if upon the source of some unwanted, disruptive distraction, he unfolds his hands and stretches out his legs.

'I'm tired.'

'Tired!' she bellows. 'You never *do* anything. I shove, but you never act. How can you be tired?'

'I've been tired for years.'

'And just what are you tired of? What, Tom? Work? Life? Me? Us? What?'

Once again he retreats into silence. Hands folded, waiting for the fit to pass.

'Look at you. More dead than alive. *You're* tired?' She bangs her chest with a sinewy fist, her eyes wild, her frame small and bony, but her presence filling the whole room. Tenacious. 'I'll tell you about being tired. I wake up wrung out. Every morning. One wretched day after another. No energy for anything. Head thumping. Heart drained. And you sit there and tell me *you're* tired. I drag myself through the hours. Day in, day out. God, it would be so blissful just to slip away from it all into peaceful sleep. But I stay alive for you. And you come home and slump in the armchair saying *nothing*!'

She lunges forward, murder in her eyes and sudden fear in his, and slaps his face as if trying to slap the dead back into life. 'Look at me!' She waves her trembling hands in front of him. 'A mess. Oh God, I can't bear this.'

She lurches to the table and grabs a knife. He springs from his chair, grabs her hands and takes the knife from her, and she sinks to the floor, sobbing, and he kneels beside her, her head on his shoulder.

'Oh Vivie, Vivie. What *have* we done?'

'Well, it's done and that's that,' she stammers.

'Yes, but *what?*'

She looks at him through tears, as if explaining the blindingly obvious. 'We dived in. We took the leap. No complaints.'

'No.' His voice deep and resonant, a slow tolling funeral bell. 'But look at you. And look at me. This is where the leap ended.'

They fall into huddled silence. At this point he stares at the knife, noticing for the first time that the blade is retractable. A stage knife. She watches him, giggling through her tears.

'Selfridges.'

'Oh, Vivie.' He shakes his head.

She stares at him as if upon a mystery. Unknowable. 'Why,' she asks, baffled, 'do I have to drag you into life?' She sighs, wrung out. 'Oh God, my nerves are shot tonight. Shot through.'

'You're shivering.'

'It's cold.' She looks up at him, trusting like a child. '*Is* it cold?'

He shakes his head. 'No.'

She nods. 'No, of course not.'

'I'll make you tea.'

She stares blankly out the window as he rises and puts on the kettle. Faint pub sounds rise from the street.

'Did you like my Effie and Lol?' she asks vaguely.

'Yes. You do a good Effie and Lol.'

'Did you like the teeth?'

'Yes.'

She looks down at the floor, wiping her eyes, the tears gone. 'I liked that bit.' She looks up, smiling. 'You can have it.'

He nods, the barest hint of a returned smile. 'Thank you.'

The kettle boils. He makes tea, pours it while she kneels on the floor, her dress all around her, and brings her a cup. As she accepts it she looks up, a pleading tone in her voice. 'Why, why Tom, do I have to explode to get you to act? Why do I have to put a bomb under you?'

He sighs, palms out, a gesture of helplessness, then retreats to the kitchen, where he sits and idly flicks through some lecture notes as if that might retrieve some fragment of the evening. She sips, gently leaning backwards, head uplifted, allowing the liquid to flow through her, feeling the soothing effects of the tea. 'Huh,' she grunts. 'You don't have to answer straightaway.'

Sounds of cheerios and ta-tas rise from the street as the pub closes. She looks to the window, speaking slowly, dreamily, as if the ghost of some long-ago, distant, suffering thing were speaking through her. 'Goo'night Effie, goo'night Lol. Goodnight, ladies, goodnight, sweet ladies, goodnight, goodnight ...'

Who were they? Vivienne stares out over the all-too-familiar night-time scene of the Harrow on the Hill shops, pondering the question. Who indeed? For they seem like strangers now with whom she was once intimately associated. He the lost soul; she one of the kindred lost – shivering, nervy, forever on the brink. That little flat of theirs they shared in another life, a place of shrieks and silence. Cold retreat and moments of tender exchange that could almost be called happy.

And outside, London Bridge falling down, falling ... The towers of the city collapsing, birds, bats and cinders swirling round in a fiery sky. A vision shared by two kindred lost souls. For she knew then as she knows now, with absolute certainty, that among the shrill cries, the shrieks, the silence and the sobbing and the tender exchanges that could almost be called happy, she was witness to, midwife to, there at the birth of, something tremendous.

* * *

Harrow on the Hill is under sleep. Harrow on the Hill is dreaming. She watches from her room, the curtains drawn back. Ghosts were out and about tonight. The ghosts of themselves, the Tom and Vivienne they were, the ghosts of all those long ago drinkers (who Tom gave new names to along with their new teeth) and all the good ladies. Re-enacting old scenes, going over old battles. Again. One more time.

She retires to her bed, the dog curled up in her basket, and switches her lamp off. Indeed, who were they? In dreams she soothes her distant self, calms her distant Tom. They dived in, they landed, and they became what they were, for better and for worse, the sordid and the tremendous wrapped round each other. Goodnight Tom, goodnight Vivie. Goodnight, goodnight ...

10.

Maurice Haigh-Wood

'You mean she's on the loose?'

'Yes.'

'Good on her! Gave them the slip?'

'Something like that.'

'Good old Vivie.'

Stephen is sitting in the office of Maurice Haigh-Wood. In the City. A broker. And, it seems, not a particularly good one. Though Stephen's visit was about his sister and her famous husband, he seemed, at first, more interested in talking about some of his own well-known blunders.

'It's a kind of fame, don't you think?'

Stephen decides that no answer is the best answer as he contemplates Mrs Eliot's brother. Talks like a twit. Looks like a twit. Toffy type. But it comes across like a bit of an act. And there's something about him that Stephen can't help but like. As though the whole upper-class-twit routine is some sort of mechanism, a way of negotiating the world. Like Mr Eliot's three-piece suit, bowler hat and brolly. If everybody's distracted by the grown-up-public-schoolboy act, then they won't look too closely at the reality. Whatever the case may be, it's impossible not to like him, for what comes through almost immediately is the emotional tug his sister has on him. Stephen can almost see them as they were, big sister and little brother, one of those bonds that never fully goes away.

'When was the last time you saw her?'

'About a month ago. A sort of farewell for a while. I'm going away soonish. Work.' He smiles. 'Business doesn't stop for war.'

'Neither does police work.'

Mr Haigh-Wood nods. 'Life goes on.'

'How did she seem?'

'Remarkably good.'

'In what way?'

'In every way.' He pauses, formulating the next part of his answer. 'Almost serene. For Vivie, that's remarkable.' He taps his desk with a fountain pen. 'Odd thing, but it's as though that time in the home gave her the chance to collect herself. Get a grip on things. Get a grip on herself. It was a different Vivie. One I've never seen before. One I would never have thought possible. She's always been at war with life. With the world. But not that day. She had … a calmness, an air of acceptance that was completely new. And unexpected. Complete change from when she was first committed. Makes you wonder if she *really* had to go in.'

He sighs, staring out his window over the business and financial district of the City, seemingly unaware of the fact that he has dropped the act.

'If you don't mind my asking, sir, who did commit her?'

Maurice Haigh-Wood exhales. 'Well, there you are. It's all a bit of a blur, really. We'd all been up most of the night. She'd been brought into the police station, babbling the maddest things. Some plot to behead Tom or something equally outlandish. I can't remember exactly, something like that. The most fantastic stuff. Her eyes, her eyes were … well, mad. Nobody could make sense of her. I felt like I barely knew her, and never had.' He stops, gathers himself. 'I saw the trenches. I'm not easily shocked. But I was that night.'

'Did Mr Eliot sign the papers?'

'Not that I recall. I think he was in the country. Cotswolds somewhere. With friends from America, I think. There may have been a phone call. It was all very confusing. He didn't oppose it, though. Not that I remember. The doctors recommended it. Almost insisted. Did I sign the papers? I can't remember. I may have.'

He drops the pen, sighs as though still burdened with some invisible albatross and stares down at his desk, contracts and letters strewn across it. 'It's a terrible thing. I really can't remember. Nobody had had any sleep, Vivie was raving, the doctors were insisting she was a menace to herself, unsafe out there alone. There were papers everywhere, forms and statements. You hardly knew what you were signing or whether you did.'

Here he rests his head in his hands, the whole episode still disturbing. The tug still there, and, no doubt, that nagging feeling that he may well have let his sister down, just as the world has. 'I suppose she could have gone to this rest house in France she'd been to before. For a month or two. Might have done the trick. Same result, who knows?' He sighs. 'Maybe it was all for the best in the end. I tell you, when I last saw her, she was as sane as anybody. A different Vivie. One I could never have imagined.'

Stephen doesn't believe the stuff about the papers; surely you'd remember that. You'd remember committing your sister to an asylum. But her brother believes it, or wants to. While Stephen is contemplating this he's also noting once again that Mr Haigh-Wood seems oblivious of having dropped the act. As though the real Mr Haigh-Wood has stepped out from behind the routine. Suddenly he looks up at Stephen, his mood lightening.

'But she's definitely out?'

Stephen nods. 'Somewhere.'

'Good old Vivie.' He scrutinises Stephen as if seeing him properly for the first time. 'And it's your job to find her?'

'Yes.'

'Well, Detective Sergeant …'

'Minter.'

'Minter. Don't expect me to help you.' He smiles. 'If anyone deserves a life, Vivie does.'

'She had help.'

'Don't look at me. If I'd been given the chance I would have. But I wasn't.'

Stephen nods. 'Have you heard of the Lunacy Law Reform Society?'

'Can't say I have. Quite a name.'

'They spring people from places like Northumberland House.'

'No, really?' He seems intrigued.

'There's an old law that says if someone can stay out in the world for thirty days and prove they can look after themselves, they're sane – if the court says so.'

Mr Haigh-Wood's smile broadens. 'She could walk free?'

'She could.'

'That would put the wind up Tom.' He speaks as if sharing a family secret. 'He's terrified of her. Never understood her. Never knew how to treat her. Vivie's not your usual woman.' He pauses. 'So, Viv could walk free. Unless you find her?'

'There's that possibility.'

Maurice Haigh-Wood leans back in his chair and breathes deeply as if on the air of hope.

'I took her a present when I saw her. When we'd said all we could find to say – she knew it was a sort of goodbye, and given the times, who knew when we'd meet again – I took an apple from my coat pocket and handed it to her. Her face lit up.' He stops and gathers himself, the memory of it still strong.

'I suppose you could say it was a sort of peace offering. I didn't have to explain myself. She understood perfectly.'

Mr Haigh-Wood gazes out the window in silence, quite possibly dwelling on his sister's smile and reliving the childhood scene now hanging on a gallery wall in Bury. Then he rises and Stephen rises with him. At the door they shake hands.

'Where are you off to?' Stephen asks.

'Kenya. Business.'

'Bon voyage.'

'Thank you.'

'When?'

'In a little while.'

'Nice time to be getting out.'

Maurice smiles. 'I fought in the last one. That was enough. I'm too old for all this. Not again.'

Stephen hands him a card with his name and telephone number. 'If she gets in touch, and she just might, call me.'

'I couldn't promise that, Detective Sergeant. This is Vivie we're talking about. Have to say I'd be more likely to help *her* if she does, and I just might have the contacts.' He raises his eyebrows, still smiling. 'Sorry. Family's family.'

It is all said with a kind of jaunty candour, a mixture of upper-class presumption and loyal little brother. He looks down at the card. 'I'll keep this all the same. No harm.' He breathes in, and sighs. A hint of satisfaction. 'So, she's out there. Our Viv. I wouldn't underestimate her, Detective

Sergeant. She looks frail. Delicate. But she's tough. Tougher than you think.'

Moments later Stephen is walking through the City: Bank of England there, Lloyds here, companies all around. All getting on with things. Indeed, he tells himself, eyeing the crowds, the sandbags and barbed wire, business doesn't stop for war. Neither does police work.

* * *

'We need to place a notice in the papers, sir.'

Stephen is talking to his chief, who nods.

'Then do it.'

'With a photograph.'

'Do we have any recent shots?'

'Not particularly. But good enough.' Stephen pauses. 'I'm not happy about it, but we're not getting anywhere. Mr Eliot certainly did not help her. Nor did her brother, although he *would* have. And Miss Purdon is lying. Wherever Mrs Eliot is, somebody must have seen her.'

His chief shrugs. 'Worth a try. Might turn up something. Or you might be swamped with people saying they saw her in all parts of the city at the same time.' His eyes narrow, the old copper smelling a rat. 'Talk to Miss Purdon again, put the squeeze on her.'

Stephen rises, closes the door of his chief's office, and enters his. Sitting at his desk he stares at the phone, impulses at odds with each other. On the one hand, he has a job to do. On the other hand, he's coming round to her brother's point of view that Mrs Eliot's suffered enough. She's got spirit and deserves a sporting chance. He's always sympathised with the fox. And he's getting to know this one.

He picks up the telephone and dials one paper after another, dictating the notice: Mrs T.S. Eliot, inmate of Northumberland House, missing. Anyone seeing her, call this number. In a quarter of an hour it's all done, the notices to be in the papers on Monday.

When he hangs up he stands at his window, watching the late Friday afternoon workers making their way home, or out, or maybe going some place they shouldn't be. There'll be criminals among those passers-by. Which ones? He eyes the soldier with his rucksack, the man in the suit with a brolly on a sunny day, that woman in the stylish summer dress, fancy necklace, who looks behind her, troubled and uncertain, as if she is being followed. He watches her, intrigued, amused. Then the smile drops from his face and he realises with a jolt that he knows her.

By the time he has run down the stairs and reached the street, there is no sign of her. Mrs Eliot has disappeared into any number of shops or into the tube. Dissolved into the city. There for one tantalising moment, gone the next. He shakes his head in disbelief. *Was* it her? He's only seen her photographs, and photographs lie. But his instincts tell him it was, and he trusts his instincts. It *was*. She's out there. He stands on the footpath, smiling. Almost saluting her. What were the chances of him standing at the window at precisely the time she passed by? Was it accident or design? If accident, what are the chances of it happening again? If design, same question.

The smile wide across his face, he scans the street one last time, then turns back inside. His fox is out there, all right. Elusive. Daring. Stylish. He mounts the stairs, his sympathy for the fox now turned to admiration.

11.

The Family Reunion

It is an afternoon show. There is a young man on a makeshift stage in a suburban church hall. He is a student. They are all students. There are a few dozen people on wooden church chairs, probably family and friends. A student production, a student audience.

The young man on the stage is playing the part of someone called Harry. But he's really playing the part of Tom. Vivienne picked that straightaway. Harry has been away for years, a ghostly, haunted figure who has just returned home. He is standing by the window of what is supposed to be a large country house up north. It is night, the curtains are open, the house a blaze of lights, its interior life visible for miles around. He is telling the various members of this family reunion, desperately trying to convince them that – fantastic as it may seem – he pushed his wife overboard, mid-Atlantic, from a cruise ship. But it's all a mystery. Tom always loved a good mystery. The rest of the family listen attentively, and with deep sympathy, but don't believe him. Did Harry really push her, or did he just imagine it?

The church is in Finsbury. Coming here was risky. Even reckless. Louise would murder her. But she *had* to see it. It's Tom's play. She's read it. She's read all Tom's writing. Always consumed by the feeling that it is all some kind of mysterious collaboration, and continues to be even though they are separated: that they created T.S. Eliot together and all his works. And always will. The poetry and the plays somehow the sum of the two of them. If she hadn't been there, making him and un-making him, destroying him and then re-creating him, he would never have written what he did. He had greatness in him, she saw that straightaway. But he had to be shoved. He had to be taken to the brink – and didn't they both take themselves there? So she's read the play, read the reviews, but never seen it because in the home they wouldn't let her out to see it. Yes, it was risky coming here, even reckless. But she *had* to.

And it's set up north, this play. Where she came from. Very telling. She smiles, while Harry, Amy and Agatha, Harry's mother, his aunt and his uncles all circle round and round the question of Harry's guilt. Because that's what it's all about. It's a very simple play, really: it's Tom feeling guilty about leaving her and doing nothing when they put her inside except going along with it. Oh, he didn't push her overboard into the Atlantic; it was overboard into an asylum. Where she might have drowned. And while once she would have taken deep satisfaction in observing that guilt, seeing it acknowledged on the page, she doesn't anymore.

And so her heart goes out to Harry, and to this young man playing Harry, and to the ghost of Tom who stands behind them. And she'd love to stand up and call out, Tom, Tom, it's all right. It wasn't all right once, it wasn't all right for a long, long time, but it is now. Was it ever just you, was it ever just me, or was our misery a collaboration too? Make peace, Tom, with the past, or like a tidal wave it will swamp you and you will drown in it. I know, because I nearly drowned myself.

She is so lost in what she might say, rehearsing words that will never be uttered, that she has been only vaguely aware of what is happening on stage. The play has gone on without her, and she now concentrates on Harry once again.

The play's chain of guilt is beginning to break. Harry is emerging from the foggy deck where the deed may or may not have taken place. But not before one final confrontation. Vivienne watches the action intently. And at first she can't quite believe what she is seeing. In one of those stage moments likely to leave an audience either laughing or gasping, a curtain is drawn back and Harry's pursuers, the Furies, who have hounded him from the tropics, across half the world, to this country house in the north of England, suddenly appear at the window. Stifled giggles and struck silence are distributed throughout the audience in equal measure. For there they are, the Furies, the Eumenides, the Kindly Ones, staring back at the players and the audience alike, wearing the masks of cartoon characters: a pig, a mouse and a rabbit with a carrot.

The giggles stop, the silence lingers, and the steady stare of these cartoon Furies, as they eye the players and the audience in the dark, becomes commanding. Vivienne smiles. How splendid! The gods of retribution, the Furies, more sinister than ever for being cartoon creations, and yet never so laughable – gods directing human fate while chomping on a carrot. She will never be able to look upon those familiar cartoon animals in the same way again. For she can imagine being pursued by just such a collection of Furies. Gods never so laughable, cartoon creations never so sinister.

At least this is what Vivienne is thinking as the makeshift curtain comes down and the audience applause does its best to fill the hall. Then the curtain rises, the players taking their bows.

The players then come down from the stage and mingle with their fellow students, friends and family. Harry is all smiles, as if he's never known a moment's guilt in his life, while he talks to a young woman he seems to be trying to impress, and for a moment Vivienne's both anxious and sad for the two of them, for no good reason apart from this sinking feeling of everything re-enacting itself, over and over again. The Furies have taken off their cartoon masks and they're laughing with their friends, as if to say – wasn't that a lark? And just as her heart went out to Harry, it now goes out to all these young people whom she has an inexplicable urge to save – but from what?

Quietly, softly, so as not to disturb their fun or encroach upon their moment – and not just the post-show chatter, but their moment of youth itself – she almost creeps from the hall, unnoticed, a distinct feeling of being invisible, a ghost herself.

Out in the late afternoon sun, Vivienne makes her way along a footpath becoming increasingly crowded as she heads towards the tube station. And something unnerving in the late afternoon light – neither day nor night but the uncertain, hazy, violet hours between both, an ominous sense of impending night – makes her turn and look back over her shoulder, once, then again, as if she is being followed and might find behind her on the footpath, visible only to her, the unlikely spectacle of a pig, a mouse and a rabbit with a carrot dogging her footsteps.

* * *

At her table in her room that evening, stirred by Tom's play, feeling the energy welling within her, she opens her notebook and returns to the tale of Sibylla, the American financier and all the clever, clever people at the party. So many parties came and went in those days that came and went – at once all too quickly, yet all too agonisingly slow.

Sibylla and her friend are walking home. It is three in the morning, they are walking across town, nobody about, marvelling at the realisation that all the time they were indoors at the party, night had never fallen. No darkness. It has been twilight all night, and still is. Neither day nor night, but eternal twilight. Why *is* that?

The uncertain hours. Uncertain, like Sibylla's response to the American financier. With his bulging eyes, his thin red lips and his hair plastered down, he should be ugly. But she likes him. If only he'd ... what?

The question is never resolved on the page because it never was in life. Whatever it was, that 'if only', that thing, he never did it. And she was forever trying to drag it out of him. But he always resisted, and always held it back. Until she finally gave up, and he gave up, and they started counting down the days, the 'if only' forever dangling on the page, the way it hung in the air in the rooms of all the little flats they lived in as they counted down their days.

She closes her notebook. It's good to know she can do this again. She couldn't for a long time, and it was like being robbed of a lifeline. Robbed of something vital that made the days matter. And made them pleasing too. Putting the pen to the page, forming words, lovely words, and making stories. Sibylla will now move on. New worlds await. Goodbye Harry, goodbye Tom, goodbye the Vivie that was. Time to leave the play and go; Sibylla wills it so ...

WEEK THREE

Mid August, 1940

12.

The Weekly Report

A park attendant picks up scraps and fallen leaves with his stick. He is elderly, and when he is not picking up scraps he leans on his stick like Old Father Time. And as Vivienne watches him meander about this small suburban park, she can't help but wonder what unsavoury evidence of summer nights he may come across – after the nymphs have departed and the knights have discarded their used armour along with their cigarette butts.

The park is now the possession of mothers, babies and nannies. It is mid-morning, and Vivienne sits on a bench beside Louise, who is holding today's newspaper. Louise shows her the notice in the paper, and the photograph that comes with it. Not a particularly good photograph and not all that recent. But good enough to identify her.

'I'm surprised they didn't do this earlier,' Louise says, as she folds the paper up.

'Perhaps I could get about in a veil,' Vivienne jokes, watching Old Man Time go about his rounds, 'like the grieving wife.' She looks down at her feet, the dog on its lead watching the comings and goings of the park. 'Then again, I've done my time as the grieving wife.'

Louise nods, half listening, preoccupied, it seems, with other things. 'This young detective sergeant came to the chemist shop last week.'

Vivienne turns to her. 'And?'

'He questioned me for about ten or fifteen minutes.'

'About me?'

'Of course.'

'What did you say?'

'I lied and he knew I was lying. But rest assured, I lied well.'

They are both quiet for a moment and when Louise speaks again it is with concern, no sign of the jolly girl guide playing a secret game.

'He was very interested in your blackshirt days.' She pauses, a frown and a slow shake of the head. 'I sort of let it slip. Sorry. But I'm sure he knew anyway. A very thorough young man.'

Vivienne sighs. 'That awful woman again. She's always popping up. Always getting me into trouble.' She pats the dog, then looks up at Louise. 'Does it matter?'

'It might.'

'Why?'

Louise weighs her response. 'I think he's a Jew. Not sure why, just a feeling. Had a whiff about him.'

Vivienne stares at her in silence, puzzled, as if some previously hidden aspect of her friend is now made visible. But she's hardly shocked. It's one of the things she and Tom had in common. Besides, there's a lot of it about. It's just that, for some reason, she never thought to hear it from Louise. And if she is surprised, she's wondering is it because she's always seen her friend as being just a bit more innocent than she ever was or is? Sometimes we make of people what we want of them, while they go on being themselves, oblivious of what we see. Until one day they surprise us, and we realise they were never what we thought, and perhaps we never knew them.

'Minter. Detective Sergeant Minter,' Louise continues. 'He wanted to know if you were a fascist.'

Vivienne raises her eyebrows. 'Well, the whole of the English working class is fascist if it comes to that. Any old working class, for that matter. Comes naturally to them.' She smiles. 'Did you tell him I just liked the uniform?'

'It's not the obvious line of inquiry,' Louise says, ignoring Vivienne's question. 'That's what bothered me,' she adds, almost as though thinking out loud. 'Couldn't help but wonder if he's on some sort of mission. As though he's made the whole thing personal.'

'What's he like … what did you say his name is?'

'Minter.'

'Minter,' Vivienne repeats, rolling the name round in her mouth thoughtfully. 'My own personal detective sergeant. Should feel privileged.'

Louise shrugs. 'He's young. Has a limp. Not your average plod. He's sharp. Intelligent face.'

'Do you think you can tell from someone's face?'

'Yes,' Louise says, as if it were beyond question. 'And I think he's out to get you.' She turns to Vivienne. 'You know, one for the Jews.'

'You're sure?'

Louise shrugs again. 'Just a feeling. But a strong one.' She smiles. 'I've a good nose for this sort of thing.'

Vivienne's gaze lingers on a nanny and a baby in a pram by a pond. It is a calm scene, restful to look upon. And, for a moment, she's wondering … children? What might it have been like? And while she's pretty sure she can't see it, the thought occurs to her more often now, now that it's utterly beyond her. And perhaps that's it. Not so much *having* children, as the possibility of it having gone, and the dawning realisation that it's not just Mrs T.S. Eliot who has moved on, but her body as well. And the knowledge that there are now things that she can never again entertain even the idea of. And with that comes a slight shiver. The years, the years, they slipped away, consumed by one dreadful row after another, or weeks of silence that felt like years. Until it felt as though all the years, apart from this last handful, had slipped away unappreciated, bowing out with a sigh, saying we were the years and we will never come again. Didn't you know?

Just then she shifts her gaze to the park gate as a policeman enters. Louise sees him too. They both freeze. Vivienne is suddenly rigid. Is this how it happens? The unlucky chance of being in the wrong park at the wrong time?

She looks down at the ground, murmuring to the dog. Louise follows the policeman's progress.

'Lou, where is he?'

'It's all right, he's gone to the other side of the park. Time to go.'

They rise, the dog leading as dogs do. 'Don't rush,' says Louise. 'We're two friends out for a stroll.'

At the park gate Louise faces Vivienne, a wary anxiety in her eyes that wasn't there the last time they met.

'Be careful. The game's changed. We don't know who's watching. Perhaps we shouldn't meet again until it's all clear.'

Vivienne nods. 'I'll listen for the siren. You still enjoying this?'

Louise eyes the distant policeman with a troubled frown. 'Less.'

With this they part: Louise in one direction, Vivienne towards the Harrow on the Hill shops. As she walks she carries with her the memory of the newspaper and her picture in it, and has never felt so aware of her face and the looks on the faces of people she passes. Then she asks herself: who reads the papers anyway? Who *really* pays attention? Besides, it's not a good shot. Taken by Louise in the gardens of her old flat. Tom gone a year, or was it two? Big day out to the races or somewhere, smart suit. She almost looks happy. All the same, it doesn't quite look like her. And for the first time in her life, she's thankful that – apart from some of the early shots with Tom – she's always photographed badly.

* * *

That night Vivienne is listless. The room is cramped. The past is upon her. She is in its grip. And she doesn't know why. It happens still. The past comes in like a sudden wind out of nowhere and sweeps her up, back into that flat she lived in long after Tom had gone, and long after she should have, back into the darkest depths of that dark night that swallowed the years …

* * *

A trail of black ants runs from the kitchen table, down the leg, and disappears into a dull corner of the flat. It is continuous. An ever-moving food chain. Vivienne has been observing it through the morning and into the afternoon, stretched out on a kitchen chair, still in her pyjamas. Her hair is greasy, her face and hands unwashed. There is dirt under her nails. The flat has no garden, no place for potted plants. She can't remember how the dirt got there. When was the last time she swept the floor? It is covered in dust and dog fur, puffs of fluff gathering in the corners of the room. The dog watches her from its cushion.

The whole kitchen is gradually being occupied by ants, bugs and the occasional spider indifferently spinning its web. But rather than being repulsed, she is fascinated.

She gazes upon the ants, all carrying tiny particles of food. To somewhere or other. They know. She doesn't. Very determined little things, ants. Like rust, they never pause. Or falter. Out there in the world, mighty factories make mighty things. Mightier and mightier. Ever onwards. No one – not the factory owner nor the factory worker; not the city nor the town – falters, pauses or breaks step. Ants, people. People, ants.

Her eyes rove over the kitchen in all its decay. It's only when you falter that you notice. It's only when you leave the march, desert or just fall away from sheer lack of energy or will, when you just don't believe in any of it anymore, don't believe that there is a greater purpose to all this industry, that you notice. Does the ant ever ask why? Does anything or anyone? Only those who falter. And even then you don't ask why, you just *see* it. And, somehow, don't care. The seeing and the not caring, it's all one.

She contemplates lifting her arm with the vague intention of gathering the broom from the closet, or the brush and dustpan. But why lift an arm? Or a finger? There is something of a blissful surrender to the whole process. Something so liberating in just not caring that she has no desire to give it up. Let the kitchen rot. Let the world, for that matter. Let the ants have it all. And the bugs. Let the wheels-within-wheels of the world rust, rot and grind to a halt. What of it? It is a deliriously tantalising image, the last of humanity wandering about a rust-bucket world, scratching its head. Once gleaming, well-oiled machines sinking back into the swamp. What of it?

Just as she's relaxing into the thought, into the blissful finality of no longer striving and struggling for this or that, she hears a key in the door, and with detached fascination sees it open and watches Louise step into the hallway, her eyes wide as she observes Vivienne. Speechless, her bag falls with a thud to the floor.

Straightaway she sees herself as Louise sees her. Vivienne in her pyjamas in the middle of the day, the ants, the dust, the filth. Her friend walks towards her and kneels, lightly touching Vivienne's knee.

'Vivie, time to get dressed.'

Vivienne tries to explain. 'But it's so nice.'

'What is?'

'This.'

Louise looks around the kitchen, then back to her friend. 'Vivie, you mustn't do this.'

'No?'

'No.'

'But it *is* so nice. I haven't felt this good in years.'

Louise shakes her head slowly. 'Vivie, do you trust me?'

'Yes, of course.'

'Then trust me now. Can you get up?'

'Yes.'

'You can stand?'

'Why, yes.'

'Then do it.'

Slowly, like an old woman uncertain of the strength in her legs, Vivienne rises to her feet, a triumphant smile on her face. 'There, see?'

Louise returns the smile. 'Good, now it's time to run the bath.'

'Is it?'

'Yes, let me take your arm.'

Slowly and carefully, Louise leads her to the bathroom and runs the bath. While it is running she turns to Vivienne. 'Now, off with these things. Shall I help you?'

At this point Vivienne looks at her friend with clear eyes, snapping back into life as if waking from a dream, and with the determination of a precocious child, the scent of salts and soap rising with the steam from the bath, says, 'No, I'm quite capable of undressing myself.'

Louise smiles. But the smile fades as Vivienne undresses, her thin, almost skeletal frame gradually revealing itself. Louise is shocked. And as much as she tries to hide it, it shows. Vivienne, seeing all this, looking back to the decay of the kitchen and the mystery dirt under her nails, stares at her friend, biting her lip.

'Louie, something's not right. It's not, is it?'

Louise eyes her, saying nothing, then rallies herself. 'No.'

'No.'

Then Louise takes her friend's hand, clasping it. 'But nothing that a good hot bath can't fix.'

Vivienne smiles, her head slowly shaking from side to side. 'Good old Louie. What would I do, what would I be …'

Louise lets her hand go. 'Good old Vivie. Now, in we get.'

With this Vivienne steps into the bath and sinks into the steaming water, the scent of the salts from Selfridges rising with the steam.

Louise gathers her pyjamas, leaves the room, and returns a few minutes later with a fresh change of clothes, placing them on a chair.

For the next half hour or so, while Vivienne washes her hair and soaps her body, hands and feet, she hears her friend in the kitchen – sweeping, dusting and cleaning. There is an occasional gasp and a cry, but it's the clatter of broom and brush, and the rattle of dishes in the sink, that Vivienne hears.

Eventually, she rises from the bath, feeling for all the world like some reborn Venus emerging from her shell, and dresses herself, revelling in the clean, crisp change of clothes.

When she steps back into the kitchen it has been transformed. Ants gone, floor swept, table wiped, dishes cleaned.

Louise beams at her. 'Now, time for tea and cakes.'

Outside, as they stroll down the street, a sweet breeze fans Vivienne's face. Summer leaves on green branches gently rise and fall. A green hour, bringing green thoughts. Sunlight sparkles on the gardens. Buses, their faces cheerful, like the buses and trains in children's tales, pass by. And while she's marvelling at it all and remarking on the newness and the wonder of everything, she's also quietly telling herself: that was close; mustn't let that happen again.

Together, Louise and Vivienne, arm in arm, carefree as the day, drift along the street, turn a corner, and follow their noses into the nearest café.

* * *

Good old Louie. Friend. Possibly the only friend she's got. How many friends do you need anyway? Did she think it or say it? The dog is suddenly alert, as if having been asked.

She leans down in her chair and pats the dog. Not long now, she says. Not long, and we can both get out of here. Free. She smiles, contemplating the idea as she prepares for bed, contemplating her notebooks on the table, all her letters irretrievably posted, her diaries back there in the home. The photographs, the scribbled notes. The things, good and bad, that friends and enemies might say and write about her one day. All the stuff of her life. And as she contemplates it all, she's possessed by the image of someone, possibly not even born yet, going over the stuff of her life in some library somewhere, piecing it all together. Coming up with … what? She falls into bed and switches the light off. Body tired, mind resisting. *What?*

For someday, if she's ever remembered at all, somebody may well write her story: Vivienne, the mad wife of the great poet. Or perhaps poor Vivienne, driven mad and left for dead. Or Vivienne, the long-forgotten, unacknowledged force behind the great man, retrieved from obscurity. It's a strange, unnerving idea, and not one she likes. But an intriguing one. Tom always hated the thought: someone sticking their nose into your private life and interpreting it for the world to ogle. Who wouldn't? But, and it's only just occurring to her, what if they come after her as well? When they've finished with Tom? What will they find, what will they make of her, what Vivienne will they create? The one that the documents and her letters and her diaries will confirm? How could it be otherwise? But not *this* Vivienne, here and now, the unrecorded Vivienne, bedding down in Harrow on the Hill and waiting for the new life to begin, the unrecorded Vivienne who lives her days out of sight, the ghostly presence between the documented lines.

Everything is silent: the room, the house, the street, the sleeping city outside. For a moment it's like having no body at all. No arms, legs, fingers, trunk or feet. Just a mind. She smiles, once more contemplating that figure, who is quite possibly not even born yet, going over the stuff of her life, piecing it all together into a portrait of Vivienne. One composed of the garnered facts. Everything about her. Everything, that is, except her mind. She could almost laugh. For what do they really have if they don't have that?

Her limbs relax, tiredness travels along her legs and arms and spine to her skull and the elusive mind, the mind in which she lives, that is housed there, and which nobody can know, no matter how thorough and scrupulous their research. Her eyes droop, and close. Her mind is dreaming. And her dreams are her own. Out of reach. Hers alone.

13.

Bertie

A deep blue Rolls-Royce passes along the street in silent majesty. Everybody stops, Vivienne too, in a kind of rapt wonder, at this touch of the sublime. Is there royalty inside? Aristocracy? The prime minister? She can't tell, nobody can. There is only the dark silhouette of a figure in the back seat, eyes possibly gazing upon the watchers in the street – or not. The car drifts on and out of view, leaving everyone to gape, shake themselves free of its spell, and get on with things. That's what they do, these people. Pass through your world with a cheery, calculating or breezy indifference, then leave you to get on with things.

There are some people from whom no good comes. People you wish you'd never laid eyes on. People whose damage seeps into your bones and entrails and lingers like a slow poison. People to whom, if you'd been told what would follow, you would never have spoken – but turned from, relieved to have dodged a near thing.

But nobody tells you, and their damage is never in their eyes when you first meet. Vivienne turns away from the street, from the retreating touch of the sublime, and stares at her reflection in a shop window. You become, she tells herself, the sum of all the things you were and are, all the people you've ever known, all the events you either initiated or became swept up in, for better or for worse. All the things you either did and wish you hadn't, or didn't do and wish you had. Looking back, unpicking it all and rearranging the thing that has become your life, and choosing all over again, only well this time, won't change a thing. It's futile. A waste of spirit, a waste of time. Weren't you always going to wash up on this footpath, at this hour, reflected in this shop window, a picture of regret and resignation? All the same, there are some people you wish you'd never set eyes on.

Staring back at Vivienne from the window is not the image of her husband – who is in all the bookshop windows now, and of whom she would never say she wishes she'd never met him – but the face of Bertie. Some of *his* books are in the window. For he is giving a talk soon. Lord Bertie. Sharp, clever, sparkling eyes. Jolly face. Jolly Lord Russell. The jolly, witty, laughing face of the devil himself. Not that the devil was visible when their paths first crossed.

Bertie's voice, like birds chattering in the trees at sunset, erupts from his image. His eyes, not quite his, goggle in their sockets. A shiver rolls through Vivienne. Tom caught him in one, as Mr Apollinax, not that it helped them. Together, they let the devil into their lives, and the devil went about his work.

Always charming. Attentive. Generous. Nothing a bother. Into their lives he came, and into hers. Slowly, at first.

A generous elder, all consideration, taking her by the hand and leading her gently into the wonders of Prospero's world. Then everything sped up. She was swept away. There she was, two or three weeks married, bumpy weeks, and Tom gone to America, summoned by his parents to explain himself. Tom gone, and Bertie *there*. Bubbling Bertie. Slippery Bertie, but he didn't look slippery then.

She draws herself away from the bookshop, that voice, the horse's neigh of a laugh, echoing faintly in her ears, as faint as the dimmed memories of the rooms they occupied whenever the chance arose, which it all too often did. It all happened so fast. Attentive and caring one day, all over her the next. And she welcomed it, yes, yes, she did. Flattered and excited. Hands fluttering all over her like an inspired sculptor. A lord, good heavens, a real lord. For didn't she, that distant Vivienne she is looking back on, always have a thing for lords and earls and all their kind? And at least somebody cared. Tom might have, but never showed it or said as much. Besides, he was gone. And Bertie was there. All over her, exciting. Fun. Babbling nonsense. Drawn to her. Infatuated, insatiable. Until he dumped her, and she saw, for the first time, the cold, indifferent stare of the libertine beneath the mask.

But as she sweeps up the street she knows that that's not it. That's not right. For even when he dumped her, they both kept coming back for more. And it dragged on for years. He seduced her, she seduced him, they seduced them. A game that took them to dizzying heights before she came crashing down to earth and he really did dump her forever. But even now, and it's a troubling truth, it's the memory of those tremulous heights that returns, and there's a renegade part of her saying that despite the misery and the damage she'd do it all again, just to have those heights back once more; a part of her saying that for all the talk of wishing you'd never set eyes on someone, there's nothing like the lure of old lovers. And for all the protestation, she remains wrapped in memory and feeling as though she's learnt nothing.

The spectre of old passion follows her up the street, the whole affair like stepping into a midsummer night's festivity, falling in love with a beautiful donkey and tumbling into an exquisitely mad dream, until the donkey dumps you and you wake to the cold, hard reality of the fact that you have been used. That you were a distraction between one lost love and the beginning of another. The devil moves on and leaves you to pick up the pieces and get on with things. But that feeling of being used never goes away. And once more she's telling herself, this time with new-found resolution and conviction, that there really are some people she wishes she'd never set eyes on. From whom no good ever comes.

* * *

In her room, she returns once more to Sibylla's world. It's good to have it back again. After so long. A place to go. And today, Bertie's face and laugh haunting her all the way back to Marjorie's house, she needs a place to go.

She flicks through her notebook. Fragments of Sibylla's adventures, or misadventures – if you can call them that. Episodes, perhaps? No, they're fragments. Tales of Sibylla, waiting to be finished. She likes fragments. They have intensity. You go straight to the heart of things. No mucking about. No time wasted setting the scene. Just plunge in and hope that they'll lead somewhere or come together somehow. And they usually do. It's a mystery. Tom always worked from fragments. They usually came together, most of them.

She flicks back and forth through the pages, calculating just which of these fragments to alight upon. Sibylla in a tawdry hotel, stretching her money out, and looking for stories in the drab corners of the Left Bank? Tom took her there, and she was looking for stories. He even stayed for a while. She flicks the pages over. Sibylla at a night club? Eager to dance and stuck with a young man going on endlessly about love, love, love … and Sibylla telling him that he doesn't *really* want love. That nobody wants love, she says – flicking a crumb off a table – and nobody gets it. Because, in the end, nobody *really* wants it. All she wants to do is dance. But he keeps going on and on, and she tells him again and again that he doesn't need love – he just wants to dance!

She pauses, staring out the window. Dancing with Tom, it was like dragging a statue around. No energy. No spark. She looks back down to the notebook. Sibylla at a bridge party, with Tom, Maurice and others? Except they all have different names. Sibylla caught up in a masquerade, everybody wearing the masks of different names.

Which one? Which of these fragments to alight upon and tease out until the fragment becomes a whole? In the end she alights on none of them. She'd like to throw them in the air and see how they land. Let chance decide. Or is it fate? It doesn't matter. It's the wrong night.

Slowly, reluctantly, she closes the notebook. They may be fragments, but these fragments were hard won. And she will return to them, and she knows they will be waiting, eyes turned to her the moment she opens the notebook. Eyes imploring her: what shall we do now? What shall we become? Can we *do* something, or are we destined to remain as we are? Scraps that might amount to something, but not now, because it's the wrong night.

Music wafts up the stairs from the sitting room. And straightaway she knows the hour. Marjorie always has music with a drink, or even two, at this hour. Sometimes Vivienne joins her, this kind, cheery soul who gives her shelter and sometimes shows signs of unbending, telling her guest things she's possibly never told anyone else.

Vivienne rises, the dog too, and together they follow the music downstairs, an American tune. She opens the door and, lingering in the doorway, says, 'Marjorie, would you mind?'

And Marjorie, sitting back on the sofa, turns, sherry in hand, and calls over the music, 'Come in, dear girl. Come in. Why ever, why ever should I mind?'

The music stops, Marjorie puts another record on. The record goes round and round, the music plays. American again. But clever. She doesn't like Americans – at least Sibylla doesn't and Sibylla is Vivienne. She doesn't like the way American men distrust European women, while at the same time they can't help but be attracted to them. Even while protecting their own women from being influenced by the likes of Sibylla. Evil Europe. But she likes their songs. And she likes this song in particular. Heaven, somebody's in heaven … She begins to sway to the rhythm, and Marjorie suddenly rises from the sofa.

'Dear girl, shall we dance?'

Vivienne can't help but laugh. 'What a splendid idea.'

And so they dance to this smooth American thing she can't help but like, that holds her in its transatlantic sway. Her cares dissolve; she is all rhythm and movement. Memories of dragging the statue of Tom around the dance floors of London melt, while the young man's moaning chorus about love, love, love is washed away by the music, and Sibylla gets her dance, after all.

14.

The Call

The scene inside the police station is calm. Quiet. Smoke in the air, the occasional clatter of a typewriter. The phones silent. A quiet Monday afternoon, well after five. A day in which nothing much has happened.

Stephen leans back in his chair, going over the typed notes of his interview with Maurice Haigh-Wood. Wondering if he might talk to him again before he leaves for Kenya. He can't escape the feeling that this brother might know something more than he says. The daffy exterior a good distraction.

Brother and sister. Family. Closer than they appear. Family always looks after family. Even if they don't really want to. That's what families do. *Have* to do. Take you in. That's what makes a family a family. When you need help, the family gives it.

He flicks from one page of his notes to another. Could this be it? Little brother, driven by guilt, springs big sister. Simple as that. Sometimes the truth is staring you in the face. Hiding in plain sight. Maybe, maybe not. He should speak to Miss

Purdon again too. Put the squeeze on her, as his boss says, but she'd only lie again. And Mr Eliot himself? Between them somebody knows. And all the while Mrs Eliot is out there somewhere. Walking around. Right now.

He grins. Of all the bunch, she's the one he's coming round to. And it is while he's asking himself if he really wants to catch her after all, that the phone shatters the contemplative silence of the office. For a moment it's as though a fire engine is passing through the station.

When he picks up the receiver he hears a man's voice. And there's something dodgy about the voice, like a street hustler's. Or a petty crim's; he's heard this kind of voice before.

'Hello,' the voice says.

'Hello.'

'Is this the police?'

'Yes.'

'About the notice in the paper.'

Stephen drops his notes on the desk, now listening more closely. 'What of it?'

'The woman ...'

'Mrs Eliot.'

'Yeah, that's it, Mrs Eliot. I seen her.'

Stephen pauses for a moment, registering the vague sensation that, in the end, he may not really have wanted to receive this call. 'When?'

'Yesterday.'

The caller then gives an address, adding that he watched her go into a house there. Stephen writes it down.

'Thought nothing of it. Then I seen your notice. Her all right. Toffy type. Toffy clothes. Stood out. What's the likes of her doing here? So I go back and get the house number.'

'You're sure it was her?'

'Yeah, I'm good with faces. Lousy with names. Not faces. It was her all right.'

'Can you tell me your name?'

'Why? Is there a reward?'

Stephen rolls his eyes. 'Maybe.'

'Maybe?'

'There might be a little something; if it's her, that is.'

'Oh, it is. It's her. How much?'

'We need to make sure it's her first. So give me your name and address, and we'll get back to you.'

The man tells him and Stephen writes it down, but the conversation leaves him feeling as if he's standing on some street corner negotiating a dodgy black-market transaction. And he's got no doubt his caller has done just that, and more.

He puts his case notes back in the Eliot folder. It's late in the day. He's not familiar with the address or the area and checks it in his A-to-Z street atlas. It's a drive. The caller was dodgy. Is the information as well? And although he'd rather be going home and getting an early night, he knows there's only one way to find out.

Even as he makes his way down to his car, the summer evening descending, he's once again registering a kind of regret, the feeling that it was the call he didn't want to get. That, of the whole bunch, it's Mrs Eliot he's come round to. That glimpse he had of her; he liked the look of her. You just had to laugh. There she was, his fox, moving through the hounds of the crowd as if invisible. Nobody batting an eyelid.

He's still smiling to himself as he pulls out from the kerb. Dodgy voice, dodgy type. Dodgy call? Only one way to find out. It's a drive. It would be. And what's he going to do when he gets there?

15.

Private Lives

Elyot and Amanda are fighting. Elyot and Amanda are divorced and have been for five years. But through the most unlikely convergence of circumstances, their paths have crossed. And here they are, fighting again. As they always did. George is Elyot, Vivienne is Amanda.

It is evening in the safe house and George is practising his lines for a local production of *Private Lives*. Vivienne is helping. While part of her has always wanted to be an actress, and part of her has always *been* an actress, she's also realising that she doesn't want to be one anymore. And it may well be that, for the first time in her life, she's content simply being her.

Although the fighting between Elyot and Amanda is stage fighting, about as real as a stage knife – this is a romantic comedy, after all – it stirs memories of all those degrading, draining fights that attended nearly every day of her married life. Tom withdrawing from her, listless, cold, icy fury. Emotionless. She pursuing him to the limits of their shared, furnished world. Flinging question and accusation, one on top of the other, on and on, until he'd turn upon her and the scene would descend into squalid grubbiness. And, of course, George's character *would* be called Elyot.

They are at a point in the play that calls upon Vivienne's character to smash a gramophone record over Elyot's head. At the same time it calls upon Elyot to slap Amanda's face. And although Tom never slapped her, Vivienne has no doubt there were times when he would dearly have loved to – just as she once slapped him, like someone trying to slap the dead back into life. Crash. She smashes an imaginary record over George's head. Whack, he delivers an imaginary slap. Stage fighting. As real as a stage knife. But some stage fighting, like cheap music, has power beyond what it ought to have.

She puts the script down on the sitting-room table. George slumps into a chair, quietly memorising his lines, while Marjorie, who has been acting as his prompter, tells him to repeat this line and that. Lines, lines, mere lines.

Vivienne delivered hers with just enough cardboard passion. But no more. Why go there again? She couldn't, even if she tried. Not now. But the squalidness of fighting, the waste of spirit, and the hollowness she was always left with afterwards all haunt her. And always will. Another Vivienne, another time. She's happy to help George, but did it have to be this play? The gods, she says to herself, the bloody gods of chance having a laugh again. And weren't they always cruel?

All the same, it is a pleasant enough way to pass the evening. For the evenings and days, all thirty of them, are something to be got through. And although she knows it is necessary, it has also been from the start a kind of imprisonment. Voluntarily imprisoned, yes. But prison nonetheless. So little things like this help pass the time, until she can free herself.

While she is counting down the days, numbering them, while George is repeating his lines and Marjorie is correcting him when she has to, there is a sudden banging on the front door.

They all start, stare at one another, and Marjorie tells Vivienne to retreat to the kitchen, out of sight. It is a dreaded moment. The police, it *has* to be. Nobody knocks on the door like that, in the dark. Vivienne withdraws to the kitchen. There is a second tattoo of banging, louder, more insistent.

Vivienne listens as Marjorie opens the door.

'Took your time,' a voice calls out. 'I haven't got all night.'

'I'm sorry,' says Marjorie.

'The blinds in the upstairs room,' the voice says. 'Close 'em! The light's visible for miles around. There's a war on, or haven't you heard?'

The air-raid warden. Vivienne sighs in relief. Her window, her bedroom. Her treacherous light. Not the police, the air-raid warden. Tom does that, or something like it. No, fire-watching, that's it. She can picture him, helmet on, gruff face, telling everyone to be on the look-out.

'I'll close the blinds now,' she hears Marjorie say, voice cheery.

'You're lucky I don't fine you.'

'Thank you for that.'

'Next time …' his voice trails off.

'Goodnight.'

'Is it?' comes the faint reply.

Marjorie closes the door; Vivienne emerges from the kitchen.

'Sorry, I'll see to it now,' she says, running up the stairs to her room.

Vivienne closes the blind, spotting, as she does, the air-raid warden looking up from the street below. And she can't help but wonder what he sees. A different woman from the one he spoke to? Surely a matter of small consequence in a night-long patrol, she decides. All the same, it's nosey types who take on the job. Officious types. Just the types to notice something, or think they have, and tell someone, who tells someone else, who winds up at your door.

In the sitting room George is going over his lines. Elyot and Amanda are at it again. Marjorie coaches. Vivienne apologises once more. They tell her not to worry, then retreat to the private lives of a cardboard stage couple, whose fighting, like cheap music, troubles the quiet domestic scene more than it should.

Vivienne says goodnight and mounts the stairs. Another sleep, another day. With every sleep and every day her confinement diminishes. And at the end of it all, the indistinct figure of a judge and gaoler, tossing the keys to her freedom up and down in his hands. Weighing the matter, or waiting on the gods of chance to decide for him.

She switches the bedroom light off, pulls the blind back, and peeks out into the night, half expecting to see that indistinct figure of the judge standing there, keys jangling. But the scene is desolate. The moon is on the wane. The hour is late. Mrs Eliot is mad or sane.

The tide of night washes over the street; the houses are sinking into watery sleep. Harrow on the Hill is dreaming in dreamy summer light. Goodnight, Vivienne, goodnight.

16.

Colindale

While Harrow on the Hill dreams, Stephen sits in his car in Colindale. Colindale, neither one thing nor the other. He's been sitting in the car for hours and he's had time to take the place in. He knocked on the door of the house he's been given the address for, but no one is in. There's an upstairs light on, the blinds half drawn.

If this is where Mrs Eliot has been hiding she couldn't have picked a better spot than these anonymous, uniform streets. Who'd look here? The tube isn't far off and every now and then someone shuffles by, shadowy figures heading home. None of them Mrs Eliot.

He'll give his watch a few more minutes. Whoever lives in there could be out all night, be away, or just be ignoring any unexpected callers. The sound of his knocking had carried right down the street, and the light on the house opposite came on just long enough for someone to pull the blind aside and take a peek.

No sign of an air-raid warden. Hard to imagine bombs falling on Colindale. He's been sitting in the car most of the evening when he could be at home, and he's had enough of the place. Just when he's about to call it a night and turn the ignition on, the lone figure of a woman, coming from the tube, walks towards him.

Her face is looking down, but her size is right; her hair, her clothes, likewise. The informer was on the money, though she's not so much a toffy dresser as a bit of a glamorous one. Too glamorous for this part of town. She certainly stands out. Straightaway he's convinced it's her, his fox, and his heart sinks. And he realises there's a considerable part of him that doesn't want to catch her. Job or no job. He hears the gate squeak, and as he gets out of the car, the woman turns to him and he speaks.

'Mrs Eliot.'

It's dark, but not so dark that he can't see that she's startled, even alarmed.

'Mrs who?'

'Mrs Eliot.'

As he nears the woman and gets a better look he can see that it's not her. Same size, same hair, but the face is all wrong. At least, it's not the face in the photographs.

'No,' the woman says.

'I'm a policeman,' he tells her, showing her his identification.

She looks both puzzled and relieved. But put out.

'Sorry, I didn't mean to startle you.'

'Well, you did. Dark street. Man jumps out of car. But I can assure you I'm not Mrs Eliot, whoever she may be. I'm not a Mrs anyone.'

Now standing in front of the woman, Stephen can also see that she's far too young.

'No, you're not, are you.'

'No. Can I go in now?'

He looks her up and down, fashionable coat, fur collar like a fox, but not his fox.

'It's late. You're out after curfew. Where have you been?'

'Work.'

'Where?'

She sighs, loudly enough to suggest that this is an intrusion. 'A club. I work in a club.'

'What club is that?'

'It's a men's club. I serve at tables.'

'You're a waitress?'

'I guess so.'

'You always get back this late?'

The woman shakes her head. 'No. Tonight was ...' She pauses, searching for the right word. 'Unusual.'

'Be careful,' he says, pointing to the upstairs light. 'Warden might fine you.'

She looks up. 'Oh, silly me.' Then she turns back to Stephen and smiles. 'So, who's Mrs Eliot when she's at home?'

'Somebody we're interested in.'

'Sorry to disappoint you.'

'You haven't.'

'Is that it, then?'

'Yes.'

'Well, goodnight officer. And good hunting.' She says this with a playful tone, and he could swear she's on the point of saying something more. In the end she nods goodbye, a half smile in the shadowy light of the doorway.

He turns and crosses to the other side of the street, contemplating that half smile and concluding it was more a lonely smile than a half one. He's also dwelling on the hours spent sitting in the car for nothing in the end and the waste of a night. Clouds glide over a waning moon, the street sits in darkness and shadow. And silence. It's both eerie and comforting, the way night transforms the world into something strange and dreamy. And it's while he's taking in the sky, the street, the houses and the silence that he sees it, keeping low against the house fronts on the footpath opposite.

Just stepped out of the shadows, the night its element. And straightaway he's drawn to the thing, entranced by it. He stands perfectly still, watching its progress. The thing completely oblivious of him. Where it came from, heaven only knows. Is there a park nearby, a railway cutting? He doesn't know. But it's here, right in front of him.

It's then that the fox stops and turns towards him, eyes shining in the night, the russet of its fur just discernible. And the more the fox stands there staring at him, the more Stephen becomes convinced that it's not frightened but curious. What are you? You're not me, but what? And why are you out and about? I always have the world to myself at this hour; what brings you out?

And while Stephen contemplates just what it may be curious about, he could swear that the fox, perfectly still, progress arrested, is on the point of approaching him to inquire more closely. Its eyes, clear and wild, shine green in the night under a beam of a streetlight. And he's not just struck by the animal's wild beauty, but its candour. Curious and open like no human he's met. That and the inescapable feeling that the fox trusts him, that it has chosen to bestow upon him its trust, and is not frightened. And he is left with a sense of privilege and a duty not to let the fox down.

They stand facing each other, neither moving. The fox will not approach, it feels safe where it is. But what if he was to approach the fox? And so, not sure what will happen, and not in the least afraid, for the fox means no harm, he takes one step, then another, and draws closer to those green, sparkling eyes. The fox stands its ground, eyeing this curiosity it has come across on its nightly round. Emboldened, Stephen takes one more step. He is on the road, the fox no more than ten or twelve feet from him. It lifts its nose, smelling him. Inquiring. Processing all the information its nose is gathering and drawing its conclusion.

At the same time, Stephen is sure he can approach no closer than this. For somehow he knows that if he was to take one more step, the fox would flee. No matter how much it may seem to trust him, there is a line the fox has drawn and he is right up against it. And just then, as if it has gathered all it needs to know, the fox moves, resumes its round and soon disappears back into the shadows it came from.

Stephen is left standing in the middle of the road, wondering if any of it happened or if he imagined it all. The blind in the woman's house is pulled back. She looks out, then closes it again, and still wondering if the whole thing was a dreamy vision, he walks back to his car.

Behind the wheel he turns the ignition key, taking a last look at the footpath and the street. *His* fox is out there, somewhere. Keeping low, nose to the air. Too smart for the hounds. Too smart for everyone. Curious and unafraid. And as he's contemplating the fox and Mrs Eliot, and about to pull out onto the street, he spots the helmeted figure of the local air-raid warden, slowly trudging down the street, checking the houses, looking for light, the air of a man on a pointless mission.

There is a fine, honeyed line running down the middle of the woman's upstairs window where the curtains don't quite close. A shadow seems to pass across it. A waitress, a gentlemen's club. A shadow in the window of a house like all the other houses, each one replicated in the next. The houses, the people inside them, asleep, dreaming, occupying the shadowland in which those bits of the mind that lie low during the day rise, slouch into view, and go to town.

17.

The Beheading of T.S. Eliot

Did it really happen? Or did she dream the scene up and bring everybody in it into being? Conjure them from the mires of the mind, the depths into which she had fallen? Were they all unwitting players in her dream – or she in theirs?

Vivienne is sweating, her breathing heavy after being jolted from a nightmare. She goes to the window and pulls back the blind. The clouds have fallen to earth out there, all over the suburb. A soft and silent landing. The houses are under a misty sea. Time and place, then and now, collapse. She is, at once, sitting in her room in Harrow on the Hill and marching the streets of Kensington all over again, as she was in the nightmare, sure of her mission. There she was, there she is. On the street in the dark.

A yellow moon looks down. She drifts along the footpath. The dog is at her side. A fluffy ball. They are walking to Tom's. They must go to him. She doesn't know where Tom is, but if she keeps walking, the dog will lead the way. Polly lifts her nose, sniffing the night air.

There is a plot to kill Tom and she has no time to lose. She must warn him. The dog will lead her. Her body hums with tension. Electric wave after wave. They mean to behead him. The whole conspiring world. Only she can save him. Tom can't live without her. Never could. He is vulnerable. Fragile. He needs to be protected. That's what a wife is for. If they so much as touch a hair of his head they will suffer the omnipotence of a wife's rage. For at this moment, floating along the street, the dog leading, she is all-powerful. But even as the dog sniffs into the corners of the night, sniffing its master out, she knows they are closing in.

And it is while she is summoning up her omnipotence from the moon, stars and heavens, while she is summoning all her strength for battle, that a young face suddenly looms in front of her. Emerging from the mist. Directly opposite, blocking her path. A policeman. How can this be? She has no time for this.

'Madam ...'

She stares at him, the power of her look surely enough to vanquish him. But he stays there. Where is her strength? He won't go. Fool.

'You're blocking my path.'

'Madam, stop a moment.'

He looks her up and down and she turns her gaze upon herself and sees for the first time that she is wearing her dressing gown, pyjamas and slippers. What of it? She had no time to lose.

The young policeman's face is grim. Fear grips her. The worst has happened. She knows it. She is too late.

'Have they beheaded Tom? Have they got to him before I could? Is it true?'

The policeman stares at her, as if searching for the right words. 'Who is Tom, madam?'

'My husband.' Doesn't this young fool know anything? 'T.S. Eliot. The "T" stands for Tom. He's famous.'

'I'm afraid I don't know of him.'

'Of course you do. I must find him.'

'Where are you going?'

'To *him*.' Really, this is too much.

'And where is that?'

'I don't know. They won't tell me. Nobody tells me anything.' She looks down at her feet. 'But the dog knows.'

Of course the dog knows. Everything makes perfect sense. *Now* will you just step aside.

The policeman breathes in deeply, then slowly exhales. 'Will you come with me, madam?'

'But I must find him.'

'And we will.'

'Do you know where he is?'

'Yes.'

'How?'

'I'm a policeman.'

Of course, he has been sent. Clever young policeman. Why didn't she see it? 'We haven't a minute to lose.'

And so the three of them, the wife, the dog and the policeman, part the mist and float up the street on the trail that will lead them to Tom. Holmes and Watson; Watson, Holmes and Polly. Tom would love it.

The next moment they're in a room somewhere. Maurice is there, and two men who call themselves doctors (but she's not having any of that) are asking ridiculous questions about the prime minister. Does she know his name? The prime minister doesn't matter! Only Tom does. Then they talk to the young constable. He said he would lead her to Tom, but he led her here, wherever they are. He lied. Another liar. There are liars everywhere. Nobody tells her the truth. But she knows the truth of the matter all the same: they're going to behead Tom. Perhaps they already have. And yet they keep asking about the prime minister. And what day it is. Who cares! Where's my husband? Take me to him now, you fools, we don't have a minute—

Then another policeman enters the room, carrying Tom's severed head.

'Is this your husband?'

That is when she woke. The streets, houses and shops are under a sea of blue mist. It's that time of morning when all things are possible. Nothing too fantastic. Vivienne is gazing upon the still, dark scene. A view that is now synonymous with the house she has come to. Stolen days. A view she knows she will miss, one day.

Did it ever happen? She has just dreamt it did, a dream as vivid as life, only more so, until the sight of Tom's severed head, smiling and dripping blood, saying I told you this would happen, jolted her back into consciousness and she woke, gasping for breath and sweating all over.

Is it one of those left-over fragments of the days when her mind contained mountains and mires, cliffs of fall so steep, brilliant flashes of insight and bottomless darkness? Fragments of fragmented days that were forever scattering and reassembling into ever-changing patterns before scattering again. On and on. Bits and pieces of a self. That's all she was. Solid one moment, shattered the next. Nightmare days she felt would never end, but which eventually did. But the remnants of them, nonetheless, live on in dreams of things that happened or didn't. Who can know now?

She leaves the window and climbs back into her bed. The bed is warm. The image of Tom's severed head fades. The fragments come together and form the Vivienne she is at this very moment, the moment to which she now surrenders, asking no more than this. She brings her knees to her chest under the cocoon of the blankets, gently rocking back and forth. All is well. Harrow on the Hill is dreaming. Her eyes grow heavy. And slowly, gently, she rocks herself back to sleep.

18.

TTFN

He's late. When he enters the pub he sees her right away. And although he's late he pauses a moment before approaching her. She's absorbed in a newspaper, pencil in hand. She doesn't look up; she hasn't noticed him come in. She is, he muses, herself. The way she is when nobody is looking. He read somewhere, a novel he can't remember at the moment, that this is the definition of reality. Imagine a table in a room when you're not there, and that's reality. He didn't care much for the novel – Mrs Woolf, that's it. But he remembered that line. And if that's true, is *this* a glimpse of the real Brigid? Alone. Herself. Brigid in a room when you're not there.

He's impressed with her power of concentration. Whatever she is reading, she gives herself over to it completely. She is not distracted by the conversations and occasional laughter around her. A rare quality.

He walks towards her and as he nears she looks up and smiles, putting the paper down on the table.

'I'm sorry,' he says.

'What for?'

'Being late.'

'Are you? I hadn't noticed.'

He smiles and sits. There's something different about her. But he can't pin it down. Her hair is the same. Dark. Fringe. Eyes, sharp as usual. Lips … lips … And then he realises that she isn't the one who is different, he is. He's looking at her differently. Anew, possibly. And realising, or perhaps just admitting to himself for the first time, that he could easily fall in love with this woman. But the thought troubles him because he has a strong suspicion that he might be the only one to fall in love. And it's not just that they're from different worlds or that she's out of his league. For there was something in her at that moment, a picture of someone who wanted for nothing, complete as she was, that made her feel unreachable, as if he was trying to grasp a shaft of light or plant his feet on the horizon.

'I couldn't help but admire your powers of concentration. What are you reading?'

'Oh,' she says, laughing, 'I'm not reading. I'm doing the crossword.'

He looks at her with a sense of intrigue.

'You like solving things.'

'Don't you?'

'It's my job.'

'It's my passion.'

It's not just the word but the way she uses it that brings a fresh smile to his face. For just as there was a sense of privilege in observing her alone, there's a similar feeling to hearing this. She's telling him things, this new friend of his. Revealing herself. That, he tells himself, takes trust. And she's chosen to trust him.

She toys with her pencil. 'I remember the first time my father explained how these things work. Clues within clues within clues. He read me a clue and it meant nothing. Complete mystery. Then he told me the answer.' She concentrates on Stephen as fully as she concentrated on the paper, about to share something important with him. And it's exciting, listening to her, because *she's* excited. 'I can only say it was like a revelation. One mystery solved. Then I started doing them by myself.'

'And it became a passion.'

'Yes. You think that's odd?'

'No, I think it's wonderful.'

Her eyes widen, slightly distracted. 'Wonderful? Of course.'

He didn't mean to say 'wonderful' but he has and feels a little foolish, even if he doesn't quite know why. Until he realises that he could almost have been saying that *she* is wonderful. Which he was.

'Thirsty?'

'Parched.'

'Beer?'

'Yes.'

At the bar he orders their beer then swings round, taking her in. She's picked up the paper again and is writing something down. When he puts the beer on the table she looks up.

'Thank you.'

'A pleasure.'

'No, not for the beer.' She laughs. 'You gave me the answer to a clue. The answer was "wonderful".'

'Happy to help,' he says, more drawn to her by the minute. 'What's your record?'

'Best time?'

'Yes.'

'Seven and a half minutes.'

'Sounds good. Well, more than good.'

She grins. 'It's not bad.'

She sips the beer then puts the newspaper away. 'That's how I got this new job. I did the crossword in seven and a half minutes. I was in a room of men. About thirty or so. I beat them all. It was one of the most satisfying seven and a half minutes of my life.' She pauses a moment as if taking it in all over again. 'My mother says only retired schoolteachers or postal clerks from Chipping Campden do these things and that I'll never get a boyfriend.'

'Do you want one?'

'Maybe. One day,' she says, playful. 'But certainly not the sort my mother wants.'

'What sort is that?'

'Posh,' she says, crushing the word as if it were a segment of orange. 'My mother's a colossal snob. She'd be appalled to learn I'm having a drink with a policeman.'

'And you?'

'I'm here, aren't I?'

He raises his glass. 'Cheers.'

'Cheers.'

'I think I know where you're going.'

'I thought you might.'

'Well, not exactly. But I get the picture. When do you leave?'

'Soon.'

'And work?'

'Sooner.'

'Are you going to miss it?'

'Not really. Be glad to be rid of Miss Fleming.'

'Who?'

'Mr Eliot's secretary.'

'Ah, yes.'

'Bit on the creepy side.' She sips her beer. 'We call her the lion at the gate. She fell in love with Mr Eliot when she was fourteen, listening to a recording of his poetry.' She laughs. 'Falling in love with Mr Eliot, I'm sorry, is a bit like falling in love with an elderly provincial vicar. I try to picture them together, you know ...' Here she snorts.

He laughs as well. 'No.'

'No. Some things you just can't picture. But mark my words, nothing will stop that woman. She will become Mrs T.S. Eliot the moment the first Mrs Eliot is out of the way.'

Here Stephen stops laughing and his face turns seriously thoughtful. Dramatically so.

She stops laughing too. 'What are you thinking?'

He waits a moment, as if weighing up some preposterous idea. 'Mrs Eliot had help when she escaped. What if it was the wrong kind of help?'

'No.' She shakes her head slowly. 'She's creepy. But not that creepy. Same for him.'

'You'd be surprised.'

'I'd be astounded.'

He leans back in his chair. 'If this job has taught me anything, it's that people are capable of just about anything.' He pauses, struck by a thought. 'It's in his poetry. Any man might bump a girl off. Has to, wants to. Once in a lifetime. Or something like that.'

She's shaking her head. 'Sorry. Sorry, I can't picture that either.'

'No.' He grins. 'Bit of a stretch. All the same, I might have a chat to Miss Fleming.'

'You know he's giving a talk on Monday evening.'

'Mr Eliot?'

'Yes. A library somewhere. Forgotten which one. Would you like to go?'

'Together?'

'That's the idea.'

Did he hear right? He did. She's just asked him out, and he sits savouring the moment before replying. 'Yes.'

'Good,' she says, rising and gathering their empty glasses. 'You never know, Mrs Eliot might be there.'

He looks up at her, dubious. 'She might.'

She holds out his glass. 'Same?'

'Same.'

He follows her progress to the bar. Whoever she is, wherever this leads, he's sure he's never met anyone quite like her. She swings round and returns with the beer in her hands and a bag of crisps in her teeth.

'What will your mother say?'

She drops the crisps from her mouth. 'My mother?'

'Seeing a policeman. Again.'

'Well, when I tell her we'll know. Besides,' she says, opening the packet and crunching on a crisp, 'you're not the average policeman, and you know you're not.'

'Do I?'

'I think you do. And thanks for reminding me about Mother. She's organised a dinner with my fascist cousin. Black tie, blackshirt. Like to join us?'

He smiles, a slow shaking of the head. 'That's very kind of you, but–'

'Kindness had nothing to do with it.'

'I could drive you home. Who knows how long I'll have the car? I've only got it as long as Mrs Eliot is missing.'

She laughs. 'Do you *really* want to find her?'

'It's not a matter of wanting, it's my job.'

'But *do* you?'

He raises his eyebrows and takes a long draught of beer. 'I was staring out the station window last week, just watching people pass. And suddenly, there she was. I couldn't believe it. It was like watching a fox walking through the crowd and nobody giving it a second glance. I ran downstairs and onto the footpath, but she was gone. All the way down the stairs I kept asking myself just what I'd do if I came face to face with her.'

'And you still don't know?'

He swirls the remains of the beer round in his glass. 'No.'

She crunches on some crisps, grinning. 'I'm not sure you've got much of a future in the police force.'

'Not sure I've got much of a future, full stop.'

They finish their beer. A conga line of dancers, uniforms brown and blue, cigarette smoke rising from them, has begun circling the pub. As they go they sing: *Run rabbit, run rabbit, run, run, run* ... Brigid nods towards the door and soon they're on the street.

In the car she eyes the siren switch, then gazes at the passing parade. 'She's out there somewhere.' Her face becomes serious. 'I hope she stays out there. She's found her freedom, I know she has. And if they find her they'll end it. They will. The whole bunch of them.'

The streets are a hazy, dim twilight, people like shadows, spectres even. And quiet. 'I try to imagine bombs falling on all this. It's not hard. Huh, I can picture that. You had any bombs drop on you?'

He concentrates on the road. 'Not on me, around me.'

'And?'

'It's everything you imagine it might be, only more so. The noise …' He shakes his head, trying to find the words, then gives up. 'But as long as you're hearing something you're okay. The one that kills you is silent. Well, I'm not sure how anybody knows that, but apparently it's true.'

The drive across town is easy, the mood sombre like the streets.

'Do you know what you'll be doing wherever it is you're going?'

She thinks for a moment. 'Solving puzzles.'

'You and me both.'

She smiles and tells him to turn here, then turn there, and soon they are parked at the front of her house. He peers up, looking at it, all three levels.

'You really can come in, you know.'

He shakes his head. She gets out, walks round to the driver's side, and he winds his window down.

'Monday,' he says.

'Monday.' She nods, then leans in and kisses him. Not a long kiss, but long enough. Then she steps back. 'TTFN,' she whispers, as if imparting some kind of code that only they know.

He nods, watches her walk towards her house, and drives off before she enters. TTFN. He asks himself: is that the briefest love note he's ever received or just something she says, has said before and will again at the end of nights like these?

He points the car towards the foreign land of Stepney, thoughts of Brigid, his fox out there somewhere, and what he would do if he ever came face to face with her all mingling, as the blackout falls on the city and the occasional searchlight roves across a silent sky.

19.

Interviewing Miss Fleming

Miss Fleming says nothing. She waits for Stephen to begin.

'Have you ever met Mrs Eliot?' he asks.

Miss Fleming straightens her back. Receiving the question as though it were a presumption, as if to say: have you not heard – I *am* Mrs Eliot? 'No, I've been spared that pleasure,' she finally says.

'You haven't met her but you've formed an opinion about her?'

'Yes. Is that so unusual? I have never met Mr Churchill, but I have formed certain opinions about him.'

'And what is your conclusion about Mrs Eliot?'

She looks out the office window, composing her answer. 'Well, since you ask. She's as mad as a hatter and the asylum is the best place for her. A selfish, screaming little spitfire. And I'm not the only one who thinks that. Just about everyone who's ever met her does. She has no friends.'

'She has at least one.'

'I'm pleased for her.'

'You dislike Mrs Eliot?'

She considers this a moment. 'I pity her.' Then she adds, 'And I pity anybody who has to contend with her. She made Mr Eliot's life a misery. So much so that he wrote *The Waste Land*. Have you heard of it?'

'Yes.'

She is surprised. 'Have you read it?'

'Yes.'

She looks him up and down, either re-evaluating him or not believing him. 'Well, that should tell you what sort of marriage it was.'

'It told me quite a lot, actually.'

She raises her eyebrows, suspicious. 'About what?'

'Various things.'

'About Mr Eliot?'

'In part.'

'I know what you think of Mr Eliot.'

'No, you don't.'

She stares at him directly, as if to say: don't treat me like a fool. 'Yes, I do. And you're quite wrong. He's the most kind-hearted, caring man I've ever met.' She pauses, slowly twisting a ring on her second finger. And as Stephen watches her, he can't help but wonder if the ring isn't a gift from Mr Eliot. It looks like a wedding ring, the sort of token lovers might exchange.

She continues. 'Everybody just sees the public Mr Eliot,' and here she pauses to allow the implication to sink in that she knows, indeed is privileged to know, something of the private man behind the public figure. 'And I've heard the jokes – Mr Eliot walking round like he's Westminster Abbey, and all the rest. But that's not *him*.' She hesitates, not sure she should be divulging her observation, but unable to stop herself. 'He needs that public face to keep the world at a distance.'

There's something possessive about what she says, one of those comments that stakes a claim to the heart of the person being spoken of. And she stops abruptly, as though her lips have indeed been loose and she's imagining the slowly shaking head of Mr Eliot in mild rebuke. Not just an old sort of young woman, not just a lover, if she is, Stephen muses, but a mother as well, caring for a fifty-year-old child. Or however old Mr Eliot is. He's starting not to like her, but understand her. Even sympathise with her. And any thoughts that she might have had anything to do with the escape of Mrs Eliot, for whatever dubious and shady reasons – the wrong kind of help – he has completely discounted. Still, he's glad he took the time to see her. She and Mr Eliot are beginning to emerge as similar types, this formal manner of hers another way of negotiating the world.

It's then that her manner becomes stern. 'She summoned up all the weapons of the weak, and he wasn't strong enough to resist. She was ruthless, and in the end she made a wreck of him. Now she's gone and it's left to other people to take that wreck and make it whole again.'

She nods and stares at Stephen as if to make it quite clear that 'other people', in this case, means Miss Fleming.

It is as Stephen is absorbing this that the door of the office opens and Mr Eliot steps in, his eyes falling tenderly on Miss Fleming. And for the briefest moment he sees a different Mr Eliot standing there. Not the public figure, or the great artist or Westminster Abbey on legs, not even the Missouri-born Yank posing as an Englishman – but someone else. A Mr Eliot who was there before all those other Mr Eliots took over. A look in the eyes, a tenderness that a small boy or a young man might have for his mother or sisters or brother, should he find them disturbed or distressed by something. The look of a comforter. The best of Mr Eliot. It is there in his eyes for the briefest of moments. A reflex. Spoken without speech. An unguarded public moment of shared intimacy. For as unlikely as the idea seemed to him just a few minutes ago, Stephen now has no doubt that they are in love. The silent exchange said it all.

Mr Eliot is changing before him. Like one of those modern portraits that are all angles – eyes, nose, lips and chin all over the place. It's like looking at someone from different perspectives, and all of them interesting. All the angles giving you a different view and different person. But all part of the one person. He's observed Mr Eliot the snob, the anti-Semite, the phoney Englishman, the poser and the cold-fish husband, but he's just seen him from another angle altogether. A different person. One that he could never have imagined existed. The one with the concerned eyes of the small boy or young man who has lived on through all those public roles and faces that he puts on to get through the day. The concerned eyes of the tender, protective lover – yes, Stephen has glimpsed the best of him.

Then Mr Eliot turns his gaze upon Stephen and it's the lofty public figure with disdain for this interfering policeman that he's looking at. There is no greeting. It is almost as if he is addressing a servant.

'Are you finished?'

Stephen shrugs. 'For now.'

Mr Eliot fixes him for a second with a piercing stare that takes his reply as an affront. 'We have work to do.'

'And so do I, Mr Eliot.'

'But you're finished,' and he adds, 'for now.'

'Yes.'

'Good. If you have finished your work, Detective Sergeant, we can begin ours. The day is disappearing.'

He says this as if reciting a line of poetry. And as Stephen rises and puts his notebook in his coat pocket he's contemplating dropping an unfortunate 'h', just for the sport of it all, but he's glimpsed the best of Mr Eliot and holds back.

'Thank you, Miss Fleming,' he says, turning to her.

'I hope you've learnt something,' she replies, pleased with herself.

'We're always learning.'

'We hope.'

When he leaves them they are conferring over a manuscript, heads together, a tender smile in her eyes returned by

Mr Eliot's, as if they are sharing an observation without need of speech.

Downstairs, Stephen gives Brigid a brief wave and a smile. 'TTFN.'

She grins. 'Till Monday.'

'Monday,' he adds, as if Monday can't come soon enough, then disappears through the door.

On the street, Russell Square a shady green, he's weighing up Miss Fleming's comments, and dwelling on that glimpse of the unguarded Mr Eliot: a picture composed of angles, all different, but all coming together like clues, so that when assembled they amount to a portrait of sorts. And perhaps that's the best he can hope for.

* * *

Stephen is at his desk, writing up his notes on Miss Fleming, when the telephone interrupts his thoughts. He contemplates ignoring it but eventually gives in to its insistence. The telephone always wins. There are certain facts of life: day will always follow night and so on, and as long as there is someone in the room, a telephone will always be answered.

It is another policeman on the other end of the line. A senior one, his voice cold and official, as Stephen's voice too must have sounded often enough. Stephen is informed, in clipped, unemotional language, that his parents have been interned in a camp in Surrey. They were taken there the night before.

Stephen sits, blank faced, staring out his window, gazing upon a suburban scene but not seeing it, and for the first time in his life cursing England. He is silent, and the silence is long.

'Are you there?'

Stephen hears, but can't seem to summon the will to speak.

'Detective Sergeant, are you there?'

He rouses himself. 'Still here, sir.'

'It's a shock, I know.'

'You might say that. It's also madness. They're no more a threat to England than the king's corgis.'

'Look, I'm just the messenger,' the policeman says, in a way that suggests he's doing Stephen a favour. 'But we have to trust that the people who make these decisions know what they're doing.'

Trust, it all comes down to trust. His parents have always been thankful to England for taking them in, have always trusted the country. And this, he's telling himself, is where that trust has led them.

'Sir, do we know the official reason? Why they've been detained?'

'Well …' the man pauses, there is a rustling of paper in the background, 'it seems they went cycling a few days ago – past an RAF base. Under their classification they shouldn't have been near one. Someone saw them, and reported it.'

Stephen shakes his head. 'Sir, this is nonsense. They're not spies.'

'No, I dare say they're not. But what can we do?'

'Can I see them?'

'I'm not sure that's possible.'

'Sir, they're getting on in years, and they will be very frightened. I need to see them. Surely we can at least be granted that.'

'I'm not so sure of that.'

'Sir,' Stephen says, a tone of one policeman talking to another, 'we both know that if you make a request, a special plea, then it *is* possible. I only need half an hour. Just to calm them because they will need calming.'

'Well,' the voice at the other end says, a mixture of the grumbling and the understanding, 'I'll see what I can do. But no promises.'

'Thank you, sir.'

They both hang up and Stephen stares down at his notes on Miss Fleming. But he's lost the thread. Or the will, or the interest. He rises and goes to the window, opens it and leans out. And there, hovering in the near distance, shining against the blue summer sky, is a barrage balloon. It wasn't there the day before, he's sure. Or maybe it was. The sort of thing that you don't notice anymore. A new kind of normal. Maybe it's been there all the time. And it's only today that he's really taken it in. Balloons hovering in the air, his parents locked up like spies for the crime of going cycling. Everything, a new kind of normal.

* * *

A disused factory on the outskirts of Dorking. Stephen left the office soon after his superior telephoned back, saying it was all very unusual and don't ask again, but yes, he could visit, after all. For half an hour.

He is sitting in his car, gazing upon the soulless sight of an abandoned brick factory. A wire fence has been erected all around it and soldiers are on guard at the front gate. His parents are in there: his father, already showing signs of age in his late fifties, and his mother, who's always fussed over him, no doubt fussing over him all the more now.

After the guards let him through he is taken to what appears to be a kind of waiting room and told to sit at a table. Nobody speaks to him; there is no sign of concern or care anywhere. He sits in silence, contemplating the pain in his knee – which fluctuates depending on the day, and for no apparent reason – telling himself there are worse things to have than a pain in the knee. And it is while he is contemplating this that his parents are led in by an armed soldier. His father may have been showing early signs of ageing before, but now he seems dramatically older. As though a decade of living has been rolled up into a few days. And his mother too, somehow more frail, but, he tells himself, perhaps it's just the fact that he's looking at her in this room with an armed soldier at her side, and another on guard at the door.

When they see him they rush towards him, and, whether permitted or not, they all embrace, his mother bursting into tears, his father just short of them. These are his parents, he's telling himself. His mother and father. They brought him into the world and guided him through it until he was old enough to guide himself. And now they rush to him, like children to their parent. And he realises that this is how it will be. Our parents were once children and will be children again, and we who were their children will become their fathers and mothers. We were their responsibility and they will become ours. And at this moment, Stephen feels the weight of that responsibility.

His mother, wiping her eyes, sits. His father, chest heaving, does likewise. And for a moment they simply stare at one another, a family again, at least. Then his father says, matter-of-factly, 'They came at night.'

'And we weren't frightened, not really,' his mother chips in.

'They were very polite. They just wanted to talk to us. Something about an air-force base. I didn't know what they were talking about,' his father adds.

'We trusted them …' his mother continues.

'So we went.'

'Why shouldn't we? This is England.'

'And then,' his father says, looking around at the room, 'they brought us here. Why? We love England. England gave us a home when a new home was needed. We wouldn't lift a finger against this country. Why are we here?'

'There's been a mistake.' Stephen knows why and knows it wasn't a mistake, but this is the best he can offer. 'Somebody, somewhere, made a mistake. And we're going to do everything we can to correct it.'

Here his father turns to his mother and says, 'There, I told you, Stephen will know.'

But his mother isn't convinced. She shakes her head. 'Can you really leave these places? We've only been here a day, but it seems like years. Don't you feel it?' she asks of Stephen. 'It's a place you disappear into and never leave.'

'Mum,' Stephen says, the very word somehow changed utterly, 'don't talk like that. People do leave these places and we're going to do everything we can to get you out. But it may take time; governments move slowly.'

His mother eyes him quizzically. 'They moved quickly enough when they brought us here.'

'We will get you out. There has been a mistake. It needs to be corrected.'

Here his father puts his arm around his mother and says once more, 'Stephen knows. We have to trust him.'

His mother nods, sighing. 'We can't even sleep together. Men here, women there.'

And it is then that the soldier who led them in approaches the table and tells them that time is up.

They stand, a family again for a moment, and hug one another. Europeans, Stephen tells himself, hug. The English have other ways around such moments. And, for that moment, he feels distinctly *un*English. But he takes heart in observing that his parents are calmer. More composed. Less like children, and more like his mother and father.

They are led away. They wave. They are gone. And soon he is seated back in his car, gazing upon a disused factory on the outskirts of Dorking. His parents trusted them, he's telling himself: those who came in the night, the authorities, the whole country. They trusted them all with the trust of children. And this is where their trust has led them.

20.

A Delicious Affair

Do you remember that weekend, Tom? I wonder. It was like having the most delicious affair with a stranger. A weekend away. A place in the country where nobody knows who you are. And soon, neither do you. Tom wasn't Tom, Vivienne was no longer Vivienne. We stepped back and two strangers took our place.

We became 'they', we shed our everyday selves with our clothes, and like some Adam and Eve hungry for sin dived into a garden of earthly delights, somewhere in Devon. Not so much a stolen season as a stolen weekend. A dirty one. I offered you a dirty weekend, Tom, and for once you followed – and together we slipped into the dirtiest days we ever knew. Don't you remember? We entered those few days hungry for sin, and left them nostalgic for it.

And so the happiest days we knew were when we stopped being ourselves – threw those two people away, Tom and Viv, threw them away into the corners of a sleepy bed-and-breakfast with our clothes and went naked for the weekend.

Became strangers. New to each other. Strangers whose tangled paths crossed in the tangled wood of that room where we let ourselves go for once, and happily *fell*.

And when the weekend was over, and the drive back to London had begun, those two strangers – mile after dispiriting mile – gradually became husband and wife again. Mr and Mrs Eliot. Familiar. All, all too familiar. Edgy, silent, then snappy. We drove back into the dead-end of Kensington, Baker Street and Bloomsbury, back into all-consuming, time-wasting, draining lunches and dinners with Woolfs and Sitwells and Fabers, endless, hollow chatter about art, art, art … and that glorious, adulterous adventure faded with every day and every night. And those two strangers we'd invented, the naked Adam and the naked Eve, were driven away by the relentless everyday world, back into their shady Eden somewhere in Devon, brooding and waiting to be summoned up again. Hungry for sin, fall and expulsion all over again. But there were no more dirty weekends.

It only ever happened once. For there can only ever be one fall. Everything else is repetition.

So how could you say, Tom, as you did often enough, that you could not find one single good, happy memory in all the years – when we had *that*? It wasn't all struggle, and it's *not* true what they say, that you only remember the good things. Sometimes it's just the opposite, and we need to be reminded of them. If I could talk to you now, Tom – now that I'm ready – I'd say exactly that. And more. That you made my life unbearable, and that you made my life possible. And I you, and yours. Because what's life for if it doesn't take you to the brink? Give me the brink every time.

Whatever it was that possessed us – and let's not call it love, for *there's* a word that needs to be publicly executed – it took us to the edge. But look, your Vivie has come through. Moved on. We destroyed each other; we made each other. And there's no point moping over what might have been. The wreckage we left behind us is for others to sift through now, all those biographers and scholars who will inevitably descend on every scrap of paper and faded photograph. And in it all, let them find hints and intimations of the brink we went to that *they* dare not approach. We had the spirit to *live* it. Grant us that much. That and the good times, which are too easily forgotten.

* * *

The dog is sleeping in her basket. Harrow on the Hill is dreaming once more. Memories are revived. Ghosts are afoot, reliving old battles and old triumphs. For there was triumph in there, as well as despair. If she could tell Tom this, she would. Don't say there are no good memories, because we both know there was good – even in the midst of nightmare. Even in those dark, dark nights of the soul we went into and from which we felt we would never emerge. Those nights when it was always three in the morning and the clock had wound down. Even then.

She can now see the whole experience with a clarity that she never could have then. Not so much like looking back on the life of two strangers, but yes, like looking back on two people whom she was once intimately associated with.

But how to let him know? For this is all she wants of him now, to let him know that all is well. That she is well, she has come through and moved on. That he can tell the Furies to go away, tell them that they are wasting their time on the wrong man. That he can stop haunting himself, and let be. Just let be.

On her bedroom dresser is a pamphlet saying Mr T.S. Eliot will speak at the London Library this coming Monday evening. 6pm. Be early. She shakes her head slowly. As much as she would love to turn up, out of the blue, have five private minutes with Tom at a public event and tell him all this – and five minutes is all she'd need – she can't. She'd never get near him. He wouldn't let her; *they* wouldn't let her. They'd grab her and throw her back inside, and the last three weeks would all have been for nothing.

The dog snorts. Whimpers. The dog is dreaming. Her favourite toy bone beside her in the basket. Vivienne remembers a game they played. She'd give the bone to the dog and say, 'Take the bone to Daddy.' And the dog would run to Tom on the other side of the room and deposit the bone at Tom's feet. Every time. The dog knew exactly what to do and never tired of the game.

And as she gazes at the sleeping dog and the bone, wistful then sad, she suddenly smiles. Of course. So simple! There all the time. Sometimes these things are staring up at us, plain as day, and we just don't see because we're looking away. Polly is sleeping, but Polly's hour is at hand. Go to Daddy, go to Daddy ... The dog will understand.

WEEK FOUR

Late August, 1940

21.

Polly

The walls of the library are lined with books, up to the ceiling, volume after volume. Folios, documents and bound manuscripts. The air is as thick with thoughts, old and new, as it is with smoke. With its classical cream colours, richly grained wood panelling and sturdy columns, the place has a sense of permanence that belongs to another age.

And just as the library is jammed with books and folios, it is also filled with readers, come to hear Mr Eliot: civilians, soldiers, flyers and sailors; English, Canadians, Indians, Australians and more; the men and women in the large open space seeming to Stephen to be a cross-section of the city at this moment. All come for Mr Eliot. He looks around, surprised. He expected a crowd. But not this. In a very real sense he is only just realising what a very public figure Mr Eliot is. For this is the kind of turn-out reserved for national leaders, heroes, actors and royalty. He and Brigid are on chairs in the seating area. Others stand wherever they can, leaning against columns or walls. A low tobacco fog fills the air along with an electric sense of anticipation.

For a moment Stephen is distracted, his mind not on the crowded scene around him, but on a soulless room outside Dorking. Brigid notices, her face a mixture of the puzzled and concerned.

'Are you all right?'

He swings round to her, apologetic, both surprised and pleased that she has read his mood. That she is attuned to him. Or seems to be. 'Yes. I'm all right.'

She's not convinced. 'You're sure?'

'Sure. It's just a family matter, nothing that can't be fixed.' He takes her hand, gives it a reassuring shake, then lets go.

'You *can* tell me.'

'Another time.'

She gives him a tiny nod. 'Another time, then.'

They leave it for now and return their gaze to the scene around them. The crowd emits a collective hum, as if an orchestra were about to strike up. The doors shut. The library, not so much large as solid, can hold no more. Everything falls silent. A distinguished middle-aged gentleman steps forward, announces himself as the president of the library and welcomes everybody. Behind him, the distinguished dead look down upon the scene. For it's not only the air of permanence that is impressive and oppressive; it's the feeling of being surrounded by tradition. Of having the many faces of tradition looking down on you. Evaluating you. One moment finding you wanting, the next reserving judgement. A hungry tradition too, one that gives every impression of constantly evolving and moving on, restless, changeless and changing, the volumes of the established that line the walls constantly rubbing shoulders with the past or making way for and accommodating the new. Each being continually changed by the other: the past influencing the future, the present changing the past. Tradition that is both constant and never stands still.

When the president has finished welcoming everyone, he assures the audience of a special evening. The greatest poet of the age will speak. He then looks behind him and introduces Mr Eliot, who has been standing behind the president the whole time. In his business suit and tie, and with his handkerchief meticulously arranged in his breast pocket, he had a kind of invisibility. Just anyone. But when he steps forward to the lectern – tall, thin, stooped and grave – he acquires a kind of grandeur as he arranges his notes, transforming from just anybody into the unmistakeable figure of T.S. Eliot.

Brigid, Stephen notices, stares at Mr Eliot as if looking upon him for the first time, as if, somehow, never having connected Mr Eliot at the office with T.S. Eliot. Well, not properly. The way the children of the famous suddenly realise at a certain age that they are, indeed, the children of the famous.

The audience breaks into applause, loud and sustained. Mr Eliot peers out into the smoke-filled space, squinting, almost pained, and waits for the applause to fade. When it does he coughs briefly, sips from a glass of water – and with no preamble, no greeting, goes straight to the heart of the matter.

'I have visited the village of East Coker, in Somerset,' he says, his enunciation precise and chiselled, his bearing almost regal, 'only once, but it is, nonetheless, a village of special significance to me.'

He pauses, coughs – a heavy smoker's cough – then continues. 'It was from East Coker in 1669 that my ancestors set out for the New World. It was a long and dangerous journey. The boat was old and leaking,' he says, stopping as if picturing the scene. 'There were those who wanted to turn around and return to East Coker, but, in what was a collective act of faith, they decided to press on and trust in God. When they finally set foot on land again it was in the New World. The Old irreversibly behind them.'

The library is hushed and Mr Eliot seems barely aware of the audience. Stephen is drawn into his tale, Brigid likewise. His voice clipped and correct. More English than the English, and once again Stephen is wondering how you get a voice like that. The whole thing is a performance. An act. But convincing. Like listening to a practised liar. Or someone so used to an adopted role that they've forgotten ever adopting it. At the same time, Stephen is noticing that although Mr Eliot barely acknowledges the audience, his gaze seems to fix momentarily on some distant point at the back of the library, a puzzled, distracted, almost incredulous look in his eyes.

'There are,' he continues, looking back to his notes, 'Eliots buried in the graveyard of East Coker, but just where is difficult to say now. The gravestones have been worn smooth by centuries of wind and rain, making them unreadable. These are the Eliots who never made that journey, having already been under earth before the boat set sail.' He draws breath, an almost haunted look about him, one for whom family history is both an anchorage and a weight. 'To the best of my knowledge I was the first Eliot to retrace the journey, from the New World back into the Old.'

Here he leans back, a storyteller who has reached a break in the story, pausing, waiting for the right moment to resume. But, at the same time, distracted by something at the back of the library.

* * *

As Vivienne enters the library, the attendant looks at the dog she is carrying in a way that leaves her in no doubt that, in normal times, dogs are not allowed. But these are not normal times. They eye each other for a second, long enough for Vivienne to let him know that she is not a woman to be messed with.

The attendant waves her through and she steps into the library for the first time. She is impressed. It's classical. Solid but oddly imposing. No everyday suburban library. Designed, Vivienne imagines, to make the simple act of entering it a civilising experience. Or a test. Or perhaps it's just designed to make you feel humble, the way cathedrals do. Or are meant to. And it is already almost full. But she can still see the lectern from the back as most of the people in front of her are seated.

Everyone is packed in, crowding the ground floor and leaning in from the gallery on the next level. So many people. It takes her by surprise, but, of course, it shouldn't. Tom *is* a public figure now, a sort of talking statue. The great man of letters. T.S. Eliot. One part of her eyes the audience – all clutching copies of his work, all eager to hear the great man – with a sceptical, even amused air. The other part takes pride in it all, the part that would dearly love to tell everybody that she, the lady with the lap-dog, wasn't just there when T.S. Eliot was created, didn't just watch as the great poet found his voice, but pushed him, shoved him, sculpted him, so much so that he grew into his name and became this public figure, at once everybody's possession and nobody's, near and distant: a demi-god in a three-piece business suit.

As she's thinking this she hears the library doors closing behind her and turns round to see the excited faces of those who've just scraped in and the faces of the disappointed on the other side of the glass. And she can't help but think of this as an apt encapsulation, a summary of the effect that Tom and all his kind had on people, back in the days when they were the young, brash newcomers – when there were those who were in on the game, and those who always felt locked out.

The library is suddenly hushed. Everybody leans forward, with an air of concentrated anticipation. A man, the president of the library, Lord somebody or other, steps up to the lectern, welcomes everybody and introduces Tom. It is a long introduction, a homage really, almost as if he were introducing Coleridge or Wordsworth. When he is finally finished he says the magic words, 'T.S. Eliot', and the crowd breaks into long and loud applause.

When Tom steps up to the lectern she is shocked. She hasn't seen him for years, and this is not *her* Tom. He is pale and thin and stooped. When did that start? He never stooped when she was around. His eyes are drawn and tired, his face pasty. He doesn't look well at all. No sign of a woman's touch there. And, at the same time, she's acknowledging the toll of their years together, not only on her but on him. Oh yes, Tom, on both of us. We made each other and we destroyed each other, broke under the strain one day and put ourselves back together the next, a constant cycle of creation, destruction, creation ... and among it all we created T.S. Eliot. But at what cost? At what cost, dear, dear Tom. You don't look well at all.

Then he starts talking about the village of East Coker and his ancestors. She isn't listening to what he says – she's heard the story before – but to the voice itself. A tired voice. You're not an old man, Tom, but you sound like one. And it crosses her mind that he might even be a lonely one. He looks it. And on impulse, to cheer him up, perhaps even put a smile on the face of the statue, she raises the dog aloft. She's at the back of the library, but she is sure Polly is visible from the podium.

'See,' she says to the dog, 'it's Daddy!'

Whether it's because she's being spoken to, senses the excitement in Vivienne's voice, or whether she recognises Tom, the dog's tail is suddenly wagging furiously. And at the same moment Tom pauses, is silent for two, three, four, five seconds, and Vivienne could swear he's spotted Polly in the crowd. But instead of bringing a smile to his face, it's as though he's seen a ghost.

* * *

Mr Eliot, as if still contemplating the fact of being the first Eliot in over two hundred years to reverse the journey and travel from the New World to the Old, gathers himself before reading the poem – his dedication to the place where everything begins and ends, or ends and begins.

Here, Stephen can't help but notice, his voice changes again, like an actor adopting a voice consistent with a part. This is clearly his poet's voice. It is not only the words he reads that tell you you're listening to poetry, but the voice itself. He sets the scene: crumbling houses, open fields, peasants, beasts – and medieval dancers, suddenly appearing, dancing in a circle to pipe and drum. The whole village, like one of those places from a storybook that can only come to life for one day in every hundred years, doomed or blessed, never to change or grow old.

Stephen, Brigid, the library, all fall silent as if under some spell: Mr Eliot the magician, his poetry the magic words.

There's something in the way the words fall from Mr Eliot's lips, like a medieval priest commanding the congregation's attention, that is hypnotic. And as though the village is taking shape before them, peasants rise from their earthy graves, dancing with heavy feet in the summer evening air. Beasts long dead munch on long-dead grass. A bonfire, centuries extinguished, crackles back into life. And soon Stephen is not even consciously listening to the words, but hearing them as you would music.

And it is while he is both fascinated by the magician's trick and also trying to work out just how the trick is done, that an odd thing happens. A dog, a small brown silky terrier, bursts through the legs of the crowd, scampers towards Mr Eliot and drops something at his feet. Straightaway, the spell is broken. The audience erupts into laughter. The priest looks down and up, puzzled. The congregation is grinning. Slipped from his control. The dog, tail wagging, looks up at Mr Eliot expectantly.

Everybody is laughing and smiling – Stephen, Brigid, the whole library. But not Mr Eliot. His eyes are wide. He is frozen to the spot. Almost, fantastic as it may seem, terrified. Turned to stone. As though some other all-powerful magician has struck him dumb.

Just as the laughter is fading, the dog barks, and the library bursts into laughter again. The event is transformed, and the crowd, having come to hear the great man speak, now finds itself watching some vaudeville routine – a man and a dog.

Or watching the solemnity of a wedding turn to farce, the guests drunk on laughter. Stephen peers closely, looking at the object the dog has dropped at Mr Eliot's feet, and sees it is one of those toy bones owners buy for dogs. And there seems to be something, perhaps a piece of paper, wrapped around it, tied with string or a ribbon. The dog barks again, the crowd laughs – although the laughter is weaker, the humour of the spectacle wearing thin – and Mr Eliot, slowly emerging from his struck state, looks up and around, as if wondering where on earth he is and who these people could possibly be.

It is then that a woman's voice calls out from the back of the library, commanding the audience's attention.

'Polly!'

Everybody turns towards the direction of the voice, then back to the dog. Mr Eliot, no longer looking at the dog, but staring out over the crowd to the back of the library. Face drained, eyes terrified, as if, indeed, having been summoned by a ghost.

At the same time the dog turns in the direction of the woman's voice, then back to Mr Eliot. Back then forward, back and forward. Confused. Desperately wanting to do the right thing but not knowing what to do. The eyes of a child torn between following one parent or the other. A whimper comes from the dog, somebody sighs. If a dog could cry, Stephen imagines, this one would. And it is while the dog is looking back and forth, waiting for the game it has played countless times over the years to resume, and for Mr Eliot to pick the bone up and give it to the dog so it may return with its prize, that the woman's voice calls again.

'Polly!'

This time the dog, hearing the urgency in the woman's voice, turns and darts through the crowd to the back of the library, leaving the bone and the note wrapped around it at Mr Eliot's feet.

Until now Stephen has been smiling and enjoying the spectacle, as you might the comic relief in an otherwise serious play or film. But the smile falls from his face as the name of the dog, Polly, booms in his ears like a giant tolling bell. And he is instantly on his feet and moving, as quickly as his leg will let him, through the crowd to the back of the library.

When he reaches the doors, there is no sign of the dog or its owner. He checks again, making sure he has missed nothing, then tells the attendant to open the door and goes outside into the evening. Negotiating the steps, he is soon standing on the footpath, looking up towards St James's Church in the distance, and sees them – a woman and a dog, as though out for an evening walk.

He follows, but they are moving quickly and he has to work hard, weaving around the few scattered pedestrians, until he eventually catches them, and as he touches the woman on the shoulder, he says her name.

'Mrs Eliot.'

The woman stops, his fox turns, and they are suddenly face to face.

'Oh,' she says, her voice resigned, accepting the inevitable. 'You found me.'

* * *

She's thinking about that voice of his as she strides along the footpath. That 'I am reading my poetry' voice. That 'Coleridge and I' voice. She wishes he wouldn't do it, but he always has. And as she mulls over it, conceding yes, yes, as poetry goes it's pretty good, she also can't help but think that his best is behind him. The early things that grabbed you by the lapels and dragged you in could only ever have been written by her Tom. But all that earthy peasant-and-milkmaid stuff is the sort of thing that anybody could write, more like a lecture than a poem. The sort of thing that someone writes when the spark is gone and all that's left is the craft. And it is while she is wondering what Tom will think if he ever reads the note, a short one, just to say she's all right, you can tell the Furies to stand down, and yr poem, it's not bad, but it's nothing on what we did together, that there is a tap on her shoulder and she hears a man's voice say 'Mrs Eliot'.

* * *

There is a garden, a small park of sorts, at the heart of St James's Square. An oasis of green in the grey. And beside the entrance, a wooden bench.

Vivienne sits on one side, Stephen on the other. The dog is in the middle.

'So,' Stephen says, admiring the terrier, 'this is the famous Polly.'

Vivienne pats the dog, still on her lead, and rubs Polly's ear. 'Are you going to take me in, turn me in?' she asks, almost indifferent. 'Or whatever it is you people do?'

'It's my job,' he says. 'The government doesn't pay me to interpret the law, only carry it out.'

Vivienne continues to pat the dog, the same offhand tone to her voice. 'Louise will be so annoyed.'

'Miss Purdon?'

'Yes. She'll be so cross. All I had to do was lie low for a few days more and I'd be free. There's a law, you know. An old one that says–'

'Yes, I know.'

'Just a few days more and I'd be free.'

'If the judge says so.'

Vivienne looks out over the square, the summer evening light fading.

'Yes, there is that to consider.'

'There is.'

'Might all have been for nothing in the end, anyway. Louise will be so cross, but I *had* to come tonight.' She pauses. 'Who told you about Polly?'

'Miss Purdon.'

'I suppose she told you Polly was our child, the baby Tom and I never had, or something like that.'

'She did.'

Vivienne gently ruffles the dog's fur. 'Our little go-between.' She leaves the dog be and folds her hands. 'When they put me back inside I'll have to say goodbye to Polly.' She sighs. 'I've long since said goodbye to Tom, and that was hard enough, but saying goodbye to this little dog will be ...' She trails off, a slight shake of the head.

As she talks about Mr Eliot, the separation – long ago, no longer an issue – the dog, Northumberland House, the beauty of this calm, still summer evening, even in time of war, and aren't those roses splendid, what strikes Stephen is not so much what she says as the way she says it. His fox is speaking to him. Calmly. Matter-of-factly. Almost serenely. Resigned to her fate. And as he is watching and listening, her brother's words come back to him. Sane. As sane as you or me. More so. And he has to agree. It's not an act. Not a pretence. No, this is a woman who has lived through some dark, dark night of the soul, one that must have seemed never-ending, and finally come out the other side – poised, a touch of serenity about her. Almost not of this world. Like a nun or a monk upon whom blessedness has fallen and who now sees the world differently.

And in that moment he feels less like a policeman and more like an accidental judge, who, through unusual circumstances, has acquired the power of Yes and No. It is not his job, he tells himself again, to interpret the law. For if every policeman made the law bend to his conscience, where would the law be? All the same, circumstances have conspired to lead him to this square, this park bench, this particular evening. Just the two of them. Nobody else. And he can't help but feel that this is one of those moments when what is law and what is right can be made to come to a private arrangement that no court would admit. Or no court that Stephen has ever sat in.

'What was in the note?'

Vivienne turns to him, puzzled. 'The note?'

'Wrapped around the dog's bone.'

'Ah,' she says, 'that note.' She raises her eyebrows. '*That* was the whole reason I came out tonight. Just to let Tom know. It's all right. I've moved on. He can stop feeling bad. We both can.'

Stephen nods, smiling. 'A peace offering.'

Vivienne scrutinises Stephen. A look that says, did I hear that right? Does he mean what I think he means? Yes, he does. 'My,' she finally says, 'you *have* done your homework.'

'It's my job.'

The two of them sit silently on the bench, the dog looking from one to the other, Stephen and Vivienne staring into the gathering twilight.

'Well,' says Vivienne, 'let's get on with it and get this over and done with.'

'Get on with what?'

'Your job. You are here to take me in, are you not?'

'Am I?' he asks, posing the question more to himself than her: what is the law and what is right?

'You said as much.'

'Did I?' Stephen asks vaguely, distracted by his thoughts, staring at her, weighing imaginary scales. Breathing in, breathing out. A man on the brink. A decision, he knows, that will change not only the life of Mrs Eliot, but his as well. The scales shift, list to one side, then the other. His mind moves upon silence. Somewhere a dog howls; Polly lifts her ears.

'You don't mean to say,' Vivienne asks, barely able to say the thing she's thinking, 'that after all this you're just going to let me walk home?'

He eyes her, curious. 'Where *was* home, by the way?'

She smiles. 'Harrow.'

He nods, as if to say: we would never have found you.

'I actually learnt to like it,' she adds, almost fondly.

'Go home to Harrow, Mrs Eliot.'

Vivienne stares at him, scarcely believing what she hears. 'Go home?'

'Yes,' he adds, 'but don't stay there. Do not put yourself before a judge at the end of your thirty days. I know a few things about trust, Mrs Eliot. Sometimes we can put our trust in the order of things, and in the goodness of our country, just a little bit too much. Believe me, I know. From personal experience.' He speaks emphatically. 'They will put you away.'

'What are you saying?'

Stephen pauses, considering deeply the outrageousness, the gravity, the consequences for both of them, the preposterousness of what he is about to say, before uttering it. 'Disappear, Mrs Eliot.'

Her face inclines towards him, incredulous. 'Disappear?'

'Yes, it happens more often than you think. Do not put yourself at the mercy of the authorities. They will have none. Disappear.'

She is stunned. 'Where? How?'

The doors of the library open. The reading is concluded and the audience spills out onto the square. Among them he sees Brigid, looking about her, frowning and puzzled, and realises they have only seconds left.

'The where is your choice. The how is more difficult. But not *so* difficult. Not with a little help. You will need a new name. And papers, perhaps. But not necessarily. People disappear, just vanish all the time. It happens more often than you think. Invent a life story. Husband dead. No children. A new start. A new life. This war is going to last a long time, Mrs Eliot, and they're not going to come looking for you. Not when I'm done. Believe me.' He pauses a moment. 'Your brother has contacts. Good ones, I suspect. Use them. He will help you with the money.'

'Tom controls the money.'

'Your brother will have to take over. But he must be the only one to know about this. Not even Miss Purdon. And certainly not your husband. He has contacts, but all the wrong ones.' He hands her his card. 'You may need this.'

Brigid suddenly spots him, waves and begins approaching. Stephen stands.

'Disappear. Now.'

With this Vivienne rises, glancing at Stephen warily, as if suspecting that this is all some sort of elaborate trap.

The dog leads. Together Polly and Vivienne walk swiftly out of the square and into the hazy twilight, spectral figures, shedding one life and walking into another, then vanishing round the corner and gone.

'Who was that?'

Brigid is standing beside him, eyes puzzled, full of questions. Stephen contemplates the corner Vivienne and the dog just disappeared around, then turns to Brigid. 'Mrs Eliot.'

She stares at him, the barest hint of a smile, an air of pleased disbelief. 'What *have* you done?'

He slowly shakes his head with that same air of disbelief as he answers. 'Indeed, *what?*'

* * *

'Disappear, Mrs Eliot.'

The young policeman's pronouncement stays with her along the footpath, not loud, but as if he is following her, whispering the same words over and over again. A whispered incantation. And as she takes his words in, the enormity of them rocks her and she is forced to steady herself. It's like being told that the only way to continue to exist is to cease to exist. To disintegrate and then take all the scattered bits of the former Mrs Eliot and mould them into somebody else. Like those missing people who just walk away, leaving their clothes and possessions behind on a beach, and are never seen or heard of again. Where do they *go*?

She stops, staring down at the footpath. The dog looks up, curious but patient. They must make an odd sight, even if there is nobody else about. But it's a passing thought. It's the business of disappearing that absorbs her. Is she ready for this, is she willing, does she even have the strength to put Mrs T.S. Eliot – Vivienne Haigh-Wood – to death? To just walk away? So that at some point in the future, who she was becomes a memory, somebody she once knew. A ghost that pops up from time to time. She did it to Tom. Had to. Turned him into a memory, so that all those feelings she'd called love would have nowhere to go and had to give up. To do that she had to kill some part of herself. Why not this?

Green Park station, sandbags stacked at the entrance, soon appears. Nobody going in or out. A lonely stop. As she approaches it the insistent whispering begins again, and she feels once more the enormity of what the young detective said. She enters the station, steps onto the escalators and descends into darkness. The tube swallows her.

* * *

Stephen and Brigid are walking back to his car. Which won't be his for much longer now.

'Sorry to just up and leave you like that,' he says, 'but when I heard the woman call the dog's name I knew who it was. There wasn't time to explain.'

'Have to say it was all very mysterious. But I thought, he'll be back. So I waited while Eliot droned on.'

'Droned?'

'Yes, definitely. Some writers should be forbidden to read their work, and he's one.'

'Well, while he was droning on I caught up with Mrs Eliot.'

She smiles. 'Quite a moment.'

'It was. And I knew from the moment she turned around and I saw that look of … resignation in her eyes, that I wasn't going to do anything.'

She raises her eyebrows. 'Has it occurred to you that you're not long for this job?'

'Might have.'

She laughs. 'I think we'll have to find something else for you.'

'We?'

'Why not? What did you tell Mrs Eliot?'

He ponders this briefly, knowing how preposterous the answer will seem. 'I told her to disappear.'

She stares at him, saying nothing for a moment, just as Mrs Eliot had herself, not long before. 'Disappear?'

'Yes.'

'Up in a puff of smoke?'

'More or less.'

'That's quite a trick.'

'It happens more often than you think. There are men and women out there living two, sometimes three lives. It happens.' He pauses. 'Mrs Eliot had a lot of faith in an old law that says if you can stay out in the world for thirty days you've proven that you're self-sufficient and therefore sane. If the judge says so.'

'And there *really* is such a law?'

He shrugs. 'Apparently. There are lots of old laws that no one's got around to fixing and have just ended up lying around. Mrs Eliot seemed to think that all she had to do was go the distance and she'd be free.'

'And what do you think?'

'They'd never let her go. I told her that. She's Mrs T.S. Eliot, for God's sake. The great man. You saw the crowd tonight. He's a sort of Churchill. They're not going to let his crazed wife go running around. Certainly not after Lord Whatsit copped his bullet.'

'So you let her loose?'

'She's been through enough. Why put her through more? What's to be gained?'

They turn a corner and his car comes into view. Brigid takes his hand and gives it a brief squeeze. 'Office legend has it that one of the girls at Faber couldn't stand lying to Mrs Eliot any more about Mr Eliot not being in, while she waited patiently with her chocolates and he crept down the back stairs. So she went to see Mr Faber. He told her to ignore Mrs Eliot and Mrs Eliot would go away.'

'Like the little man upon the stair.'

'Something like it.'

They reach the car and stand there, she on the footpath and he at the driver's side, the twilight thickening into night.

He opens the car and looks over the roof at her. 'St John's Wood?'

She nods. ''Fraid so. I haven't packed yet.'

They get in. 'What time's your train?'

'Seven.' She grimaces. 'I wouldn't blame you if you don't come.'

He grins. 'Wouldn't miss it for the world. I love railway stations at seven in the morning. I'll even bring a hanky to wave.'

'Not sure I'm the sooty hanky sort.'

He laughs as the car starts. 'Not sure *I* am.'

She eyes him emphatically. 'Yes you are. You've just proven yourself to be a rank sentimentalist.'

'We'll just make it a wave, then.'

She leans back in her seat. 'You'll have to show me your flat sometime.'

He grins. 'Stepney? You want to see Stepney?'

'Maybe.'

'Safest part of London, Stepney.' He laughs. 'Who'd want to bomb Stepney? If they ever did, they'd be doing it a favour. I'm telling you, Stepney ain't St John's Wood.'

'So I've 'eard.'

She's no sooner said this than she propels herself forward, lunges for the green button and sets the alarm off, the whole car suddenly ringing in the dull, blank street. Brigid falling back into her seat, a contented smile on her face as she looks out the window at a passing couple. 'They'll think I've been arrested.'

Not long afterwards they pull up at the front of her house, siren no longer sounding.

He turns to her. 'Well, see you at the station.'

She nods, smiling. 'Seven.'

'Seven.' He taps her shoulder. 'Don't disappear.'

'I've no intention of disappearing. Besides, we have to find you a new job.' Her smile brightens, then she leans forward, kissing him. 'There'll be more of that at the station, and after. All the afters,' she says, her laughter pealing softly on the breeze and out into the night as she opens the door. 'TTFN.'

He watches her go, turning to him and waving at the door as she slips inside the house. He sits, quietly marvelling that life is unfolding when he least expected it in unexpected ways, and that a bedsit in Stepney might not be the beginning and end of things. Stepney – he waves just for the record, a grin all over his face – the safest place in London. Who'd want to bomb Stepney?

The engine is running, the street quiet and still. The city beds down, St John's Wood and Harrow on the Hill. His fox is on the loose. Gone. Taken flight. Smiling, he pulls out into the night, then gathers speed. What *have* you done? What, indeed?

22.

East Coker

Accident or design? The bus stopped here. She got off. One minute later the bus left without her. If there's no design, what's an accident? If there is design, how can there *be* an accident?

Vivienne leaves her bag at the pub, then, with Polly on her lead, steps out into one of those summer mornings that seem to cast a spell over everything – people, animals, trees and gardens. Even the houses and buildings. The whole village lulled into a timeless doze. The clocks may have stopped, the earth's revolutions paused for a sun-drenched moment. Minutes, hours and days dissolving, mere inventions imposed upon nature to make trains and buses run on time. The pub dog doesn't even lift its eyelids as she passes. The bus, cream and orange, has departed, taking time with it.

Vivienne follows the road taking her away from the pub, which seems to be the centre of whatever this place is. Not really a village, nor a hamlet. More a sort of gathering of houses and people who happened to wind up here. There must be a shop of some sort but she can't see one.

Tom didn't talk about the place all that often, but often enough. Enough to sow the seeds of curiosity. So when she saw the sign and the bus stopped, she stopped. She follows a rough country road that leads away from the pub, barely aware of her steps, her mind more sensations than thoughts, until a cemetery, a church and green fields rolling out into the distance appear before her.

Are there Eliots here? The graveyard is weathered, the tombstones, smoothed by wind and rain, are moss brown. Old stones that can't be read. As she wanders around, the grass whispering, birth and death dates, here and there, become decipherable. And as certain dates repeat, for children and babies as often as as not, she realises she is walking among the plague dead. Babies no sooner taking their first breaths than taking their last. No wonder Tom's ancestors left.

And while Vivienne is eyeing the gravestones and the church itself, which appears to be open more in hope than expectation, she witnesses a most improbable sight and begins to seriously wonder if she hasn't stepped into another time and place after all.

There are a dozen of them, men and women. All in medieval dress. Their music precedes them. A pipe, a drum. Laughter and singing. They dance towards the church, a circle within a circle, one going this way, one going that, and at the centre of both circles she sees a couple and realises it is a wedding. Whether they have risen up from a long sleep like, indeed, the inhabitants of those villages that are cursed or blessed to come to life only one day in every hundred years, their faces, music and laughter embedded in this place, is neither here nor there. That is the way it feels. They are here, in this timeless now. And entrancing in a way that they themselves are completely unaware of.

They dance nearer. The drum beats, the pipe plays. The outer circle breaks, as does the inner. They encircle Vivienne and she joins the dance as it revolves and floats towards the church. When they reach the church door they stop. So too the drum and the pipe. She finds herself staring into the eyes of the young bride, directly in front of her, eyes bright, on the brink of the new life, wide with expectation, and she doesn't know whether to be fearful or hopeful for her. The dancing has ceased, the lovers hold each other by the hand, and disappear into the church along with the other dancers, where, for better or for worse, they will be joined in holy matrimony.

Vivienne is left standing alone at the entrance of the church, gazing around the still scene she once again occupies, when a car horn rudely breaks the spell. Her mind once again thinking everyday thoughts as a bus appears before her, and time resumes.

She collects her bag, containing a letter to Louise that says all she dares say at the moment, and is soon sitting on the bus, Polly beside her, gazing out the window in a kind of wonder at the adventure of life beginning all over again, leaving this sleepy gathering of stone and wood behind her. And all those Eliots who set out from here for heaven only knew what, all those years ago. Just as she too, quietly disappearing, moving from one life to another, has no idea where she will end up. For she has resolved to take the bus as far as it goes, to land's end, trusting in fortuitous accident or design that the road will lead her to the place that awaits her arrival, and which she will instantly recognise as her new home.

The bus follows a rough dirt road across rolling green fields, the dog by her side, the driver at the wheel. On and on, long, long into the day, until the road runs out, the land falls away, the tide rolls in, and the sea begins ...

Acknowledgements

Many thanks to the following.

Catherine Milne and Belinda Yuille at HarperCollins, my editor Amanda O'Connell, the work of Jo Butler, and my agent Sonia Land and all the gang at Sheil Land.

I would also like to acknowledge Lyndall Gordon's imaginative and astute biographies of T.S. Eliot. She really is in a league of her own.

Finally, my special thanks to my partner, fellow writer Fiona Capp – my first reader, my first editor – for her constant support, suggestions and advice, not just in the writing of this novel but all of them. And to Leo – just for being Leo.